The Play's the Thing

Book
5

Stan Rogow Productions • Grosset & Dunlap

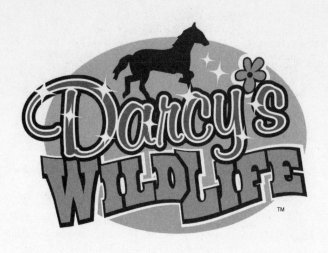

The Play's the Thing

Book
5

By Sierra Harimann

Based on the television series
created by Tim Maile & Douglas Tuber

Stan Rogow Productions • Grosset & Dunlap

GROSSET & DUNLAP
Published by the Penguin Group
Penguin Group (USA) Inc., 375 Hudson Street, New York, New York 10014, U.S.A.
Penguin Group (Canada), 90 Eglinton Avenue East, Suite 700,
Toronto, Ontario, Canada M4P 2Y3
(a division of Pearson Penguin Canada Inc.)
Penguin Books Ltd, 80 Strand, London WC2R 0RL, England
Penguin Ireland, 25 St Stephen's Green, Dublin 2, Ireland
(a division of Penguin Books Ltd)
Penguin Group (Australia), 250 Camberwell Road, Camberwell,
Victoria 3124, Australia
(a division of Pearson Australia Group Pty Ltd)
Penguin Books India Pvt Ltd, 11 Community Centre, Panchsheel Park,
New Delhi - 110 017, India
Penguin Group (NZ), Cnr Airborne and Rosedale Roads, Albany,
Auckland 1310, New Zealand
(a division of Pearson New Zealand Ltd)
Penguin Books (South Africa) (Pty) Ltd, 24 Sturdee Avenue, Rosebank,
Johannesburg 2196, South Africa

Penguin Books Ltd, Registered Offices:
80 Strand, London WC2R 0RL, England

Published by Grosset & Dunlap, a division of Penguin Young Readers Group, 345
Hudson Street, New York, New York 10014. GROSSET & DUNLAP is a trademark
of Penguin Group (USA) Inc. Printed in the U.S.A.

Library of Congress Cataloging-in-Publication Data is available

ISBN 0-448-44352-X   10 9 8 7 6 5 4 3 2 1

Hello!

I'm Sara Paxton, also known as Darcy Fields on Darcy's Wild Life. You are totally going to love the two new books in the Darcy series!

In some ways, Darcy and I are very different, but in others we couldn't be more alike! We both love summertime—cute summer clothes, warm weather, suntans—and we're both a little dramatic.

Luckily, I get my share of drama filming Darcy's Wild Life, but, now that she's been uprooted from Hollywood, Darcy sometimes has to make her own! Bailey turns into Baileywood when Darcy gets involved with the local theater production, and the possibility of a trip back to Tinseltown has Darcy caught between her two worlds. The simple life? I think not!

I've been playing Darcy for a while now, and, boy, has my character come a long way! She still misses the excitement—and a little bit of the drama—of her old life in Hollywood, but Darcy absolutely loves her new life in Bailey, livestock included! She's a natural with animals, and, with great friends and a wonderful mom to support her, is it any wonder that this girl can do anything she sets her mind to?

Life is definitely a walk on the wild side with Darcy, but you can always count on her (and me!) to make the most of it! I'm so excited about all of the adventures in store for Darcy, and I know you will be, too.

I hope you're enjoying the show, and I know you're going to love these books! Thanks for joining me, and happy reading!

Best Wishes!

♡ always,

Sara Paxton

Chapter 1

Wild Wisdom . . . *Cattle consume as much as one hundred fifty pounds of grass. They graze about eight hours each day.*

Briiing! The bell above the door to Creature Comforts clanged as Darcy Fields entered the veterinary clinic. She tossed her sparkly pink backpack in the corner.

"Wheeeeee!" she cried, grabbing her friend Lindsay's hands and spinning her around in a circle. "It's summer break!"

Lindsay smiled at her friend as she tucked her reddish brown hair behind one ear.

"I know," Lindsay agreed. "I can't believe it! We have an entire summer of working at Creature Comforts ahead of us. Isn't that the best thing *ever*?"

Darcy sighed. "Actually, no. The *best* thing ever is when you find a pair of shoes that perfectly match your brand-new Miss Sixty cami. But I guess a summer at Creature Comforts is a *really* close second."

Lindsay gave her friend a wry smile. Ever since Darcy had moved to Bailey from Malibu with her former movie star mom, Lindsay had listened to Darcy lament Bailey's deficiencies: no trendy shops, no full-service salon, no yoga studio, and no smoothie bar. But deep down, both girls knew that Bailey had grown on Darcy. In fact, in the past few months, Darcy had been volunteering for extra hours at the clinic, and she had stopped mentioning the nonexistent yoga studio altogether.

As she stocked a shelf with bottles of pet vitamins, Darcy thought about all the cool creatures she had learned to treat at the veterinary clinic. She had helped out with chicks, ferrets, horses, pigs, puppies, cats, snakes, and bats (though the last two on that list had definitely *not* been her favorites).

But as much as Darcy loved working at the clinic, she was hoping there would be more to Bailey this summer than just animals. If she was going to be working at the clinic full-time with nothing else to do all summer long—well, Darcy thought she might go a little batty herself!

"So, Lindsay, I've got a question for you," Darcy asked. "What else is there to do in Bailey during the summer *besides* working?"

Lindsay cocked her head thoughtfully. "Hmm . . . Well, there's the Chili Cook-off every July. That's a real crowd-pleaser."

Darcy was unimpressed. She wasn't much of a cook, plus she wasn't a huge fan of chili. The idea of those cute cows ground up into a spicy stew just didn't appeal to her.

Lindsay looked pained as she tried to come up with something else. "Oh!" she cried excitedly. "And there's the cattle drive just outside of town every August."

"The what?" Darcy asked.

"Cattle drive," Lindsay repeated. "You know, when all the cowboys drive the cows back to the ranch after a summer spent chewing cud in the wilderness?"

"Oh, right," Darcy replied. "The cattle drive. Yee-haw." She swung her arm in a circle above her head as though she was about to lasso something.

At that moment, Lindsay's dad, Kevin, owner of the veterinary clinic, poked his head out from the back room.

"Did I just hear someone say 'cattle drive'?" he asked. He got a faraway look in his eyes that Darcy had begun to recognize as his "way back when" look.

"When I was a little boy, the cattle drive was the highlight of my summer," Kevin said. "I used to get dressed up in a cowboy hat and a pair of tiny cowboy boots and I would make a lasso out of a jump rope. Ah, those were the days."

Lindsay and Darcy giggled.

"What?" he asked. "What's so funny?"

"Just the image of you in cowboy boots and a cowboy hat, Dad!" Lindsay blurted as she and Darcy broke into a new round of laughter. Dr. Adams pretended to be hurt, then disappeared into the back room.

"Aw, man!" The girls heard a voice behind them.

They turned to find that their friend Eli had just entered the clinic. He was lifting up his feet to look at the bottoms of his shoes.

"Do I have toilet paper stuck to the bottom of my shoes or something?" he asked the girls desperately.

"Um, no, Eli," Darcy replied. "I don't think you do."

"Oh, good." Eli sighed with relief. "I just heard the two of you giggling, and I figured I had done something embarrassing."

"Now what would make you think that?" Lindsay asked good-naturedly. She and Darcy both knew that Eli could be a huge klutz. And he was no stranger to embarrassing moments, either.

"Oh, nothing," Eli responded as he plunked a huge stack of papers down on the counter. "Do you guys have a hammer and some nails I can borrow? I have to hang up these flyers around town."

Darcy looked alarmed. "A hammer and nails?" she asked. "What about this nice roll of masking tape?"

She practically shoved the tape at Eli. The thought of him with a hammer and nails made her very concerned for his safety—and the safety of those around him.

"Thanks, Darce," Eli said as he waved the tape away and accepted the hammer and box of nails Lindsay was reluctantly offering instead. "But these are printed on pretty thick paper, and I'm not sure that tape would work."

He held up a poster to show Darcy, whose blue eyes lit up.

"Omigosh!" Darcy squealed as she grabbed the poster out of Eli's hand. This was the best news she'd gotten in weeks!

The poster announced an open-call audition for roles in Bailey's annual summer stock performance. Darcy scanned the poster quickly for details and noticed that the auditions were the very next day!

"Lindsay!" Darcy chided her friend. "You forgot to mention the absolute *best* thing that happens in Bailey in the summer—summer stock!"

Darcy thrust the poster in her friend's face.

"Oh, yeah," Lindsay remarked. "Summer stock. Must have slipped my mind. I've never been really into theater."

"But this is so *exciting*!" Darcy shrieked. "Why don't you like theater?"

"I have the worst stage fright," Lindsay admitted with a shrug. "When I was in the second grade, our class did a play on the fifty states. I got to play Nevada, and I had to wear a big poster board that had the state capital and state flower painted on it."

"Poster board?" Darcy gasped. "That is so *not* stylish!"

"Um, Darcy, that's totally not the point of the story," Lindsay pointed out tactfully. "Anyway, when it was my turn to belt out, 'The capital of Nevada is Carson City,' I completely froze! It was a nightmare."

"Well, that was a long time ago," Darcy reminded her friend. "Maybe you've grown out of your stage fright. Besides, theater can be so much fun! You get to dress up and act like a totally different person."

Darcy had pretty much given up trying to convince her mom that they really belonged back in Malibu among the glitz and glamour of Hollywood. And the truth was that Darcy had learned to really like Bailey and all of her new friends here. But she still missed one thing from her old life—drama!

"I can't wait to audition!" Darcy gushed. "You should think about trying out, too, Lindsay. You can work through your stage fright. And Eli, I'll bet you could help out backstage or something. You're really great at, um . . ." Darcy searched for the right phrase. "Helping out!" she blurted.

"Yeah, thanks, Darcy," Eli replied warily. "But as you can see, I'm already helping out. I'm supposed to be hanging up these flyers, remember?"

"And thanks for the offer, Darce, but I think I'll pass," Lindsay added. "I'll definitely come see you on opening night, though."

And with that, Eli grabbed a nail from the box, positioned it at the top of the poster, and raised the hammer to strike the nail. Darcy squeezed her eyes shut, not wanting to watch. Meanwhile, Lindsay made herself very busy behind the counter.

A few seconds later, much to everyone's surprise, there were no yelps of pain from Eli. Instead, he was standing back to admire his work.

He cocked his head and tapped his chin lightly with his finger. "That's not too bad, if I say so myself," he said proudly. "I think I'll just tack another nail at the bottom so it doesn't flap in the breeze when the door swings open."

Eli raised the hammer again, this time making firm contact with his thumb.

"YEEEEEAOOWWWW!" he howled as he jumped up and down, sucking on his thumb. "Aw, man! And I thought I was doing so well."

Lindsay and Darcy both shook their heads. Poor Eli.

"I'll get you some ice," Darcy said, rushing into the back of the clinic.

"Thanks," Eli said when Darcy returned with a plastic bag full of ice cubes. "I'd better go finish putting up these flyers." He turned to go but then suddenly stopped and turned back to face Darcy. "And, um, maybe that masking tape isn't such a bad idea. Mind if I borrow it?" he asked sheepishly.

"Not at all!" Lindsay interjected as she handed him two huge rolls of tape.

Once Eli had gone, Darcy situated herself in front of the Creature Comforts computer.

"Darcy!" Lindsay scolded. "Aren't you going to finish stocking those vitamins?"

"Of course!" Darcy replied, hurt that her friend would make that kind of accusation. She tried hard to always be on task. Well, except when there was something much more exciting going on! And this was definitely one of those times. "This will only take a second, Lindsay. I promise."

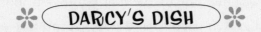

DARCY'S DISH

Major news! It's summer here in Bailey. Yee-haw!
(That's what the cowboys would say on a cattle drive,
but that's a long and kinda boring story.) Anyway,
there's even more exciting news than that—auditions
for Bailey's summer stock show! That's right, people.
You are reading the blog of the future star of a major
theatrical production. Well, at least I'm hoping to be the
star. Auditions are tomorrow, so wish me luck! And stay
tuned . . .

"There," Darcy said, triumphantly clicking to shut
the browser window. "I promised it would only take a
second."

"Thanks for the update," Lindsay said sarcastically.
"Now back to the vitamins! Chop! Chop!"

"Okay, okay," Darcy replied reluctantly, dragging
herself away from the computer. She went back to the
shelves she had been stocking. The shelves were right
above the old guy who spent his days sleeping on a
bench in the corner of Creature Comforts. Darcy had
nicknamed him Snoozie. She was so used to him being
there, she hardly even noticed him as she reached
over his head repeatedly to put vitamin bottles on the

15

shelf. He was just one of the many things in Bailey that Darcy had gotten used to and now accepted as part of her daily life.

As she stocked the shelves, Darcy wondered about the play she would be starring in. The flyer hadn't mentioned what the show would be. Maybe she would be Scarlett O'Hara in *Gone With the Wind* or Juliet in *Romeo and Juliet*.

Whatever the show is, I'm bound to make the perfect star, Darcy thought confidently. *I mean, it does run in my family!*

Darcy's mom, Victoria Fields, was a popular British film actress. Well, she *had* been an actress before she decided it would be a good idea to move to Bailey so that she and Darcy could live like "normal people." Their new life was sort of like *The Simple Life*, except that Darcy wasn't Paris Hilton, and her mom sure as heck wasn't Nicole Richie!

Nowadays, Victoria spent most of her time in her garden, tending to carrots, tomatoes, potatoes, cucumbers, and whatever else she managed to grow. Victoria had loved Bailey right from day one, whereas Darcy had taken some time to adjust. And now that she was fully adjusted, it was the perfect time to get back in touch with her roots.

My roots as a star, that is! Darcy thought, a smile on her lips.

"Hey, Lindsay," Darcy called to her friend. "Do you think there's any chance that some totally cute local guy we've never met before will show up at the audition tomorrow and land the role as my costar? Maybe the play will even have a kissing scene in it! Omigosh, that would be *so* fantastic!"

"Yeah, it might be," Lindsay agreed. "But then again, you never know who might audition, so a kissing scene could also be really, really bad. For instance, take note of our next customer."

"Customer?" Darcy asked. "I don't see any cust—"

"Ladies, ladies," a voice boomed behind her. "Haznoy is in da house."

Darcy spun around to find herself face-to-face with Layne Haznoy, one of Bailey's more colorful characters. Darcy groaned inwardly. Layne was a nice guy, but he could be a little bit over the top.

When Darcy first moved to Bailey, Layne had developed a crush on her and had made it his mission to become Darcy's boyfriend. Actually, he had proclaimed her his girlfriend while Darcy had tried desperately to dodge his affections—to no avail.

Darcy completely understood why Lindsay had

pointed out that a kissing scene with the wrong costar could be a very bad thing indeed.

"Hi, Layne," Darcy said, taking a step backward. "What do you have in there?" She gestured toward the pet carrier Layne was holding. In addition to doing outstandingly bad imitations of movie characters, one of Layne's hobbies was collecting unusual pets.

"It's a chinchilla," Layne replied.

"A china what?" Darcy gasped, looking petrified.

"Relax, Darcy," Lindsay said calmly. "It's a chinchilla. They're rodents that look sort of like chubby squirrels with big, mouselike ears. And they're really pretty cute."

"Hey, that was good," Layne said, surprised. He popped open the cage and reached inside, pulling out an adorable gray ball of fluff with *really* big ears.

"Awww," Darcy cooed. "Aren't you just the cutest little chinchilla I've ever seen? Okay, so maybe you're the only chinchilla I've ever seen, but whatever. Can I touch him?"

"Sure," Layne said. "But it's actually a her. She likes to be scratched under the chin and behind the ears. I brought her in because her eyes are looking watery and she hasn't been herself lately."

"She is *so* soft!" Darcy exclaimed. "But what do you mean, she hasn't been herself?"

"Well, she used to love rolling around in her dust bath, but lately, she just sits there and doesn't do much," Layne responded sadly.

"A dust bath?" Darcy asked, perplexed. "That doesn't exactly sound like something that would get her clean!"

"Actually, chinchillas clean themselves off by rolling around in dust instead of using water," Layne replied.

"That seems strange," Darcy said. "Wouldn't water get them cleaner?"

"Well, chinchillas are from the Andes Mountains in South America. In their native habitat, it's too cold for them to use water, so they use dust instead," Layne explained as he scratched the chinchilla lovingly behind the ears.

Lindsay leaned over to take a closer look at the furry little creature. "Her eyes do look a little watery. My dad should probably take a look at her. If you want to leave her here for a bit, you can come back and pick her up in an hour or two."

"Sounds good to me," Layne said, turning to leave. Then he opened his mouth to add something, but Lindsay beat him to it.

"Let me guess," she mused. "Haznoy out?"

"Hey!" Layne protested. "That was my line!"

"Oh, well. Sorry," Lindsay said nonchalantly. "Say,

Layne—speaking of *lines*, you aren't by any chance auditioning for a part in Bailey's summer stock show, are you?"

"Yeah, baby, yeah." Layne gave the girls his famous Austin Powers impression. "You'd better believe it. And I intend to land the starring role."

Lindsay glanced at Darcy, a "told you so" look on her face.

Darcy grimaced. "Well, good luck at the auditions," she said generously. "Maybe I'll see you there."

"Shagadelic, baby!" Layne crowed. "Haznoy out!"

Darcy sighed. Suddenly, her bright future in Baileywood seemed a little dimmer.

Chapter 2

The next morning, Darcy rose bright and early and practically sprinted down the stairs into the kitchen.

"Good morning, darling," Victoria Fields greeted her daughter. "Where's the fire?"

"Um, right behind you!" Darcy replied, dashing past her mother toward the toaster. The toast that had just popped up was charred black and smoking profusely.

"Aw, man!" Eli said from the other side of the kitchen, where he was tending to something on the stove top. In addition to hanging flyers and doing other odd jobs around town, Eli was also employed as the Fields' general helper on the farm and around the house. And breakfast with Eli as the chef was always a bit of an adventure.

Darcy fanned the air above the toaster and the smoke dissipated.

"Well, that toast will go perfectly with this tomato, cheese, and ash omelet." Eli sighed. He turned toward Darcy and Victoria, holding out a pan. The yellow egg, red tomato, and white cheese were all the same color—black.

"Not to worry!" Victoria said as she jumped up from the kitchen table. "There's a reason that frozen waffles were invented." She opened the freezer and removed a box of frozen blueberry waffles, popping two into the still-smoking toaster.

"Um, thanks," Darcy replied. "But I think I'll just grab an apple and a granola bar . . . I don't want to be late for my audition!"

"Audition?" Victoria asked. "What audition?"

"Oh, right!" Darcy said excitedly. "I was just about to tell you. Bailey has an annual summer stock theater show, and I'm going to audition for a part."

"That's wonderful, dear," Victoria said. "And what show is it?"

"Good question," Darcy mused. "I have no idea. But I guess I'm going to find out. See you later!"

Darcy raced to the playhouse, her bicycle tires squealing on the dirt path that led from the main road to the building. She propped her pink bicycle up against the horse hitching post and rushed inside, her pink helmet still perched on top of her head.

She skidded to a stop in front of her English teacher, Ms. Harrington.

"Here I am!" she announced breathlessly. "Am I late?"

"Why, hello, Darcy," Ms. Harrington greeted her warmly. "Well, if you're here for the Bike for a Cure race, you're definitely late, as that event was yesterday."

Darcy looked perplexed.

"Bike for a Cure?" she asked. Then she realized that she was still wearing her helmet. "Oh! Right!"

She removed her helmet, shaking out her long blond hair in her best movie star impression. "No, I'm not here for the race," she said, striking what she assumed was a theatrical pose. "I'm here for the auditions."

"Ah, yes!" Ms. Harrington replied. "The auditions. Then you're actually quite early. I'll be directing the play this year. Would you be able to help me set things up?"

"Not a problem at all, Ms. H.," Darcy said brightly.

�֎  �֎

Okay, quick update. I'm at the auditions now, and it turns out my English teacher is the director of the show.

Ms. H. is just about my fave teacher here in Bailey,
and I totally aced her class this year. That's sure to
help me out when it comes to scoring the lead. To be
the star or not to be the star . . . that is the question!
(I told you English class was one of my strengths!)
More later!

Darcy grabbed a few folding chairs and carried
them into the theater. Ms. Harrington had set up
a table for the judges, and Darcy set up the chairs
around the table.

"Thank you so much, Darcy," Ms. Harrington
said. "This will be perfect for me and the Brennan
brothers."

"The Brennans?" Darcy asked, a puzzled look on
her face. "I didn't know they were into theater."

The Brennan brothers were famous in Bailey
for their large collection of exotic animals, not their
Shakespearean soliloquies.

"Well, yes, I guess they do like theater," Ms.
Harrington replied thoughtfully. "But I imagine
they volunteered to help out with the auditions more
because of the animals."

"Animals?" Darcy asked. The last time she
checked, plays were for humans, not livestock and

exotic animals like the ones the Brennan brothers loved.

"What about them?" a voice said.

Darcy turned to find her friend Kathi beaming at her. When Darcy had first met Kathi, she hadn't believed one person could smile so much. But as she quickly learned, Kathi was famous for her friendliness, and she was rarely without a grin.

"Hi, Kathi," Darcy exclaimed, giving her friend a hug. "I was just wondering why the Brennan brothers are helping Ms. Harrington with the auditions. Plays don't really strike me as their kind of thing."

"But of course they are. The Brennans always help choose the animals for the Bailey summer stock show. What are you doing here? Are you auditioning yourself, or are you just here as a stage mom?"

"A what?" Darcy shrieked. "You know I don't have any kids, Kathi. I mean, I'm only fourteen!"

"Not kids, silly!" Kathi chided her friend. "Animals! I thought maybe you had brought Orville to try out for the part of Wilbur."

"You mean there are *animals* in this play?" Darcy asked, incredulous.

"Of course!" Kathi cried. "It's all about the animals. The play is *Charlotte's Web*, you know."

Darcy groaned, hitting her forehead with her hand.

"I should have known! My dreams of stardom—dashed. Who knew I would have to compete with a pig for the lead role? Call me crazy, but all of the plays I've ever seen have starred people *only*."

Kathi shook her reddish brown pigtails and laughed. "Not in Bailey! Now, is Orville trying out for Wilbur or not? I was hoping Petula wouldn't have too much competition."

Kathi gestured toward the end of the pink leash she was holding to reveal her pet pig.

"I figured Petula had a good start in theater after my dad's car commercial, and this play was a natural next step."

"Um, yeah, sure," Darcy replied. "She'll be great. And no, I didn't bring Orville."

Orville was a pig Eli and Lindsay had helped Darcy save from becoming a big slab of bacon.

"I didn't even realize there was a part for a pig," Darcy continued. "I guess now I know why they call it summer *stock*, huh?"

Darcy chuckled at her joke, elbowing Kathi in the side.

"Get it? Live*stock*?" Darcy repeated. "Come on, it's *funny*!"

Kathi laughed. "I get it, Darcy. But I hear it every summer!"

Darcy sighed. "I guess my future in comedy is looking even more dismal than my career in theater right now."

Kathi headed outside to warm Petula up for her audition, and Darcy went over to Ms. Harrington's judges' table to look at the cast list:

<u>Characters</u>
Fern (a girl age nine or ten)
Mrs. Arable (Fern's mother)
John Arable (Fern's father)
Avery (Fern's brother)
Homer Zuckerman (Fern's uncle)
Edith Zuckerman (Fern's aunt)
Lurvy (the hired man)
Wilbur (the pig)
Goose (the goose)
Gander (the gander)
Lamb (the lamb)
Templeton (the rat)
Charlotte (the spider)
Assorted baby goslings

Darcy looked up at Ms. Harrington skeptically. "You don't mean to tell me that you're actually going to audition spiders for the part of Charlotte, are you?"

Ms. Harrington chuckled kindly. "Well, no, dear. But you remember the story of *Charlotte's Web*, don't you? In the book, Charlotte can speak, the same as all the other animals. So we'll be auditioning people for voice-overs."

"I guess that's a plus," Darcy mused. "No lines to memorize! Then again, I could always try out for Fern, couldn't I?"

"Actually, I was hoping to have a slightly younger child play Fern," Ms. Harrington said gently. Then something seemed to catch her eye. She stood up from the table and strode over to Jack Adams, who had just entered the room.

"Aha!" Ms. Harrington cried. "For example, this young man is just the age of child I'm looking for to play Fern."

In addition to being Lindsay's younger brother, Jack was also the town schemer. His goal in life was to become rich and famous, and he was determined to take whatever path was necessary in order to make it happen. Jack could be slicker than a Hollywood agent, and his number-one client was always himself.

"Me?" Jack shrieked. "A star? Awesome! Who is this Fern character, anyway? Sounds like some kind of plant."

Darcy rolled her eyes. "That's because it *is* a plant, Jack," she chided. "And it also happens to be the name of one of the main characters in *Charlotte's Web*."

"Sweet!" Jack replied. "*Charlotte's Web*—sounds like a great mystery. Uh, you know—one with a really *tangled* plot." He gave Darcy what he thought was a sly and knowing showbiz wink. Then he puffed out his chest proudly. "And it looks like I'm going to be the main man in this caper—Inspector Fern."

Kathi stifled a giggle.

Ms. Harrington opened her mouth to correct Jack, but Darcy beat her to it.

"Don't you ever read books?" Darcy sighed, exasperated. "*Charlotte's Web* isn't a murder mystery. And Fern isn't a detective—*she's* a little girl!"

"A what?" Jack gasped. "I am highly insulted."

He put on a big show of being offended by the suggestion, but it only lasted a moment. Once he regained focus on his one life goal—to be rich and famous—he changed his tune.

"Then again," he mused aloud. "I could just wear a wig and use a squeaky voice, right, Ms. Harrington? I know I'll be a great star, no matter what the part!"

He smiled up at her, a beatific grin on his face.

"Well, I'll certainly consider it," Ms. Harrington replied diplomatically. "Though I must say that I have you in mind for another role as one of the animals' voices. So you may want to consider trying out for the voice-overs as well."

"What about me?" Darcy asked. "If I'm too old for Fern, which parts should I try out for?"

"Whichever ones you like, dear," Ms. Harrington answered. "I don't have anything in particular in mind for you, but don't worry. If you really want to get involved in this play, I can use all the help I can find. And I'm sure there's a role for you somewhere in this production. Now, where are those Brennan boys?"

With that, Ms Harrington wandered off to locate her co-judges.

❋ (DARCY'S DISH) ❋

Why? Why, why, WHY? Of all the plays, Ms. H. chose *Charlotte's Web*, which is full of—you've got it—animals! I mean, they're actually having a casting call for rats! Can you imagine? So, it looks like I won't be starring in this play. And even if I do manage to get a part at all, it looks like I may be sharing the spotlight with a pig! This kind of thing could only happen in Bailey.

Chapter 3

Wild Wisdom . . . *Llamas are nature's drama queens—a female llama will spit at a male llama to let him know to get lost.*

Darcy stepped outside to get some air. She was still reeling from the shock of finding out that she wasn't going to be making her theatrical debut as Juliet or Scarlett O'Hara anytime soon.

Oh, well, Darcy thought. *I suppose it could be worse. At least I won't be kissing Layne Haznoy anytime soon. And I still have a shot at a voice-over part!*

Darcy imagined herself beginning her voice-over career in Bailey and going on to do numerous commercials and cartoon characters in movies. *Omigosh!* she thought. *I could be the next James Earl Jones!*

Renewed by the possibility of a successful lifelong career as a voice-over artist, Darcy headed back to the playhouse. Then she heard a truck pulling up behind her, and she turned to see the Brennan brothers roll by in their pickup.

"Hey, guys!" Darcy called.

"Hi, Darcy," Brett replied as he pulled into a parking space. Brandon hopped out of the passenger side door and then went around to the back of the truck to let out Oprah, the Brennans' pet llama.

"Hi, Oprah," Darcy said to the llama as she patted her gently on the head, being careful not to look her in the eye. Oprah had a nasty habit of spitting at people who looked directly at her. "Ms. H. told me you guys were helping her judge the animal auditions, but why is Oprah here?"

"She's here to audition!" Brandon announced proudly. "We figured since she already has the name of a famous actress, she might as well have the chance to *be* a famous actress herself!"

Darcy shook her head in disbelief. "First I find out that half the cast of this play isn't human, and now I find out that some of the animals auditioning for parts aren't even the same kind of animals as the ones in the play! Are you going to dress Oprah like a lamb?"

Brett and Brandon both laughed. "Well, Ms. Harrington told us that she didn't mind if the animals weren't exactly the same as the animals in the book. And I don't think there were any lambs auditioning for the part of the lamb, so Oprah seems as good a choice as any, don't you think?"

Darcy threw her hands up in the air in defeat. "Why not?"

Darcy headed back inside the playhouse, where auditions were about to begin. Kathi was sitting next to Petula, whispering into her floppy pink ears like a true stage mom.

"Now, remember to smile, Petula," Darcy overheard Kathi tell the pig. "You're going to be terrific!"

"How's it going?" Darcy asked Kathi.

"Oh!" Kathi said, startled. "Uh, fine. It's not like I'm talking to a pig or anything!"

Darcy laughed. "It's okay, Kathi. I think it's great that you're being so supportive. And I'm sure Petula's going to be great."

Kathi beamed at her friend.

"Thanks, Darce!" Kathi replied. "I knew you'd understand. I figure I'm always trying to teach Skittles to do tricks, and if I can do that, why not teach Petula how to act? Or at least how to stand still onstage while someone else says her lines from backstage."

Darcy wasn't sure that she had ever seen Kathi's dog, Skittles, successfully perform one of the tricks that Kathi had taught her, but she knew it hadn't been a lack of effort on the part of her friend. Darcy just hoped pigs were smarter than dogs!

Ms. Harrington stepped onto the stage and clapped to get everyone's attention. "Welcome, everyone," she announced. "We're ready to begin. We'll be auditioning for the human roles and voices first, and then we'll move on to the animals."

"This should be very interesting," Darcy whispered to Kathi.

"Tell me about it!" Kathi replied. "Two years ago, Ms. H. tried auditioning the animals first, and by the time she got to the people, there were so many droppings on the stage that no one wanted to go up there!"

Darcy laughed. "Well, I guess it's a good thing she's doing people first, then."

"Um, yeah," Kathi responded. "I guess." She gestured to the stage, where the first audition had begun. Jack was standing in the middle of the stage, a microphone in his hand.

"For my audition, I'd like to treat you all to a song," he addressed the crowd.

"Uh, Jack," Ms. Harrington interrupted. "There's really no need—"

Unfortunately, Jack couldn't hear the rest because he began belting out "There's No Business Like Show Business."

"Ugh!" Kathi groaned, covering her ears. "Jack isn't what you would call a great singer."

"Forget about great—he's not even *good*!" Darcy pointed out. "This is the worst singing I've heard since my friends and I tried to sing 'Happy Bat Mitzvah to You' in Hebrew to Adi Abramowitz last year."

". . . Let's go on with the show!" Jack finished with a sweeping bow. "Thank you, thank you! No need for applause."

Ms. Harrington cleared her throat. "Thank you, Jack," she said kindly. "That was a very, um, *rousing* rendition of that inspirational song."

She consulted her clipboard for the next performer.

"The next person up is Layne Haznoy," Ms. Harrington read aloud.

Darcy hit her forehead with the palm of her hand. "This just keeps getting worse!"

Layne swaggered onto the stage wearing a powder blue three-piece suit with an enormous ruffled collar.

"I'll be reciting lines from the Austin Powers movies," Layne boomed into the microphone.

"Lovely, Layne, lovely," Ms. Harrington replied. Darcy thought she saw her teacher wince a bit. "And just a tip, dear," Ms. Harrington added. "There's no need to hold the microphone so close to your mouth. We can all hear you just fine."

"Okay, no problemo," Layne replied, clearing his throat. "That's not my bag, baby," he drawled in his

Austin Powers–style British accent. "I mean, really! Who throws a shoe? That really, really hurt."

Layne stuck his pinky finger into his mouth and struck a pose.

"Is that all?" Ms. H. asked him.

"Well, my ferret Mini Me would like to audition for the role of Templeton the rat," Layne said. "His audition will be the Dance of the Sugar Plum Fairy from *The Nutcracker Suite*."

Layne dashed backstage and reappeared holding a pet carrier, which he opened with a flourish. Mini Me poked his head outside of the carrier, took one look at the bright lights at the foot of the stage, and quickly retreated back into the carrier.

"If you don't mind, Layne, I'd like to audition all of the people first, and then we'll get to the animals. At that point, we'd certainly be interested in seeing Mini Me's, um, ballet."

"Sure, Ms. H.," Layne replied, sauntering off the stage with the pet carrier tucked under one arm.

As Kathi and Darcy watched, the auditions continued. Both children and adults took the stage to perform Shakespearean soliloquies, lines from movies like *The Godfather* and *The Princess Bride*, and songs from Broadway musicals. All the while, the animals waiting in the wings were getting extremely impatient. As Darcy's turn on the stage approached, the baaing sheep, snorting pigs, squealing rats and ferrets, and squawking geese swelled to a very loud crescendo.

The din was so loud that Ms. Harrington could no longer hear the woman onstage who was singing "Memories."

"Cut!" Ms. Harrington cried. "CUT!"

The woman onstage stopped singing abruptly. She looked like she was about to burst into tears. "Was I that bad?" she asked, her voice wavering. "I've been practicing for weeks!"

"No, no, not at all," Ms. Harrington reassured her. "I'm just having trouble hearing you over this racket!" She gestured toward the group of people waiting off to one side with leashes and pet carriers. The area was labeled "Livestock Audition Waiting Area."

Ms. Harrington looked around desperately for help. "Has anyone seen Brandon and Brett?" she pleaded.

"Oprah was having a spitting contest with Layne, so the Brennans had to take her outside for a time-out," Kathi informed the frazzled director.

"Oh, dear." Ms. Harrington sighed. "What am I going to do?"

Chapter 4

> **Wild Wisdom . . .** *Bar-headed geese are able to fly at a speed of over fifty miles an hour without wind to assist them. In fact, they are so strong that they can fly in crosswinds without being blown off course.*

Ms. Harrington scanned the crowd of eager thespians desperately. When her eye caught Darcy practicing her lines in a corner, her face lit up. "Darcy!" she called. "Can you come here for a minute?"

"What's up, Ms. H.?" Darcy asked eagerly. "Am I next?"

"Actually, I was hoping you could help me out with something. You work at Creature Comforts with Lindsay Adams and her dad, Kevin, right?"

"Yeah, I do," Darcy replied warily. "Why?"

"Well, I just don't know what to do to keep these animals quiet so we can finish up the rest of the auditions. And I know you work with animals, so I was thinking you might have a few ideas."

Never one to back away from a challenge, Darcy

racked her brain for ideas. She looked at the motley
crew of people and animals gathered in front of her.
Petula kept trying to bolt for the door while Kathi stubbornly tugged at her leash, keeping her inside. Mini Me
was making an incredible amount of noise biting on the
wire bars on the front of his cage. And a bunch of geese
were busy flapping their wings and squawking at another
cage that Darcy assumed housed a rat or another rodent.

Then it occurred to her—she could totally handle
this. Darcy knew from experience at Creature Comforts
that it helped to keep different kinds of animals separated
when they were in stressful situations. And based on
the butterflies in her own stomach, she figured
theatrical auditions *definitely* qualified as a stressful
situation, even for animals.

"I guess I do have a few ideas, Ms. H.," Darcy said.
Her teacher looked so relieved, Darcy felt bad for not
stepping up and helping out earlier.

"I think this livestock waiting area is too small for
all of these people and animals. It's nice outside—why
don't you tell everyone to wait with their animals
outdoors, and when you're ready for each of them,
someone will go outside and tell them to come into the
playhouse?"

"Darcy, that's a brilliant idea!" Ms. Harrington
gushed. "I don't know why I didn't think of that!"

With Darcy's help, Ms. Harrington ushered all of the stage moms and pets outdoors.

"I also think it's a bad idea to have so many different kinds of animals so close to one another," Darcy told everyone once they were outside. "Everyone should spread out by five to ten feet or so."

At that moment, the Brennan brothers reappeared with an unhappy-looking Oprah at their side.

"Sorry to abandon the auditions, Ms. H.," Brett said. "We just had to deal with Oprah. What can we do to help?"

"Actually, I think Darcy and I have it covered," Ms. Harrington responded. "Why don't you wait with Oprah right here, and I'll send someone outside to get Oprah when it's time for her audition? I just have a few more people to see."

Darcy's ears perked up. That meant her audition was definitely soon.

"Am I next?" Darcy asked eagerly.

Ms. Harrington gave Darcy a look that she definitely recognized. It was the one her teachers always used before they asked her to do something she most certainly would not be interested in doing.

"Well, Darcy, I was hoping you could stay out here with the animals and sort of take charge of things. The Brennans seem to have their hands full, and I could really use the extra help when it comes time for the animal auditions. And I'll make sure to consider you for a role, even if it means you have to audition later."

"Oh, okay," Darcy said softly. Was she ever going to get her chance in the spotlight? Darcy looked at Ms. Harrington, and she saw that her teacher looked completely stressed out. She was disappointed, but she realized that Ms. H. really needed her help.

"Sure, Ms. H.," she replied. "No problem."

DARCY'S DISH

Summer stock theater sure is harder than I thought it would be! Now instead of auditioning myself, I've been recruited to help run the auditions for all of the livestock. They say there's no business like show business, but now I'm not so sure!

Darcy slipped her PDA into her backpack. She and Kathi, Petula, and all of the other stage parents and animals had been waiting outside for at least thirty minutes.

"Kathi, can you keep watch out here for a second?" Darcy asked her friend. "I want to see what's going on inside."

"Consider it done," Kathi replied confidently.

Darcy stepped inside the playhouse. The building was a lot cooler than it was outside, and she was beginning to think that maybe her idea to bring the animals outside hadn't been a very good one.

Darcy approached Ms. Harrington at the judges' table.

"Thank you, Julie," Ms. Harrington told a small girl who had just finished reciting a few lines from *Annie*.

"Ms. H.," Darcy whispered. "When do you think you'll be ready for the animals? It's hot outside, and I think everyone's getting a little restless."

"Perfect timing, Darcy!" Ms. Harrington exclaimed. "Julie was the last human audition. Why don't you tell the Brennans to bring Oprah in now?"

"Great!" Darcy said, relieved that the wait was finally over. "I'm on it."

She practically ran back outside and led the Brennans and Oprah into the cool auditorium.

"Thanks, Darcy," Ms. Harrington said. "Why don't you stay inside just in case I need some more animal wisdom?"

Darcy watched as the Brennans led Oprah out onto center stage, where she promptly turned to face the back of the stage.

"Now let's see her face forward," Ms. Harrington instructed.

The Brennans tried to coax her into turning around, but Oprah wouldn't budge.

"Come on, sweetheart," Brett cooed. "Let's turn this way."

The llama stubbornly faced the back of the stage.

"I don't know what's going on," Brandon apologized to Ms. Harrington. "She isn't usually like this. She's always loved being the center of attention."

Suddenly, Darcy remembered the way Mini Me had reacted on the stage earlier. He had poked his head out of his pet carrier, and as soon as he had seen the bright lights at the bottom of the stage, he had retreated.

"Hey, guys!" Darcy shouted from below the stage. "I think I know what's wrong!"

"Really?" Brett asked in surprise.

"Yes!" Darcy sprinted onto the stage. "Doesn't Oprah have to wear a sleep mask in order to fall asleep at night?"

"Well, yes, but what does that have to do with this?" Brandon replied.

"I think the stage lights are too bright for her," Darcy answered. "That would explain why she won't face forward."

Darcy turned toward the front of the stage. "Ms. H.!" she called. "Can we turn down the lights at the front of the stage?"

Ms. Harrington signaled to the guy in the control room, and the lights dimmed.

Brett tried getting Oprah to turn around again, and this time it worked!

"Thanks, Darcy!" he said. "You really helped a lot."

Next, Kathi and Petula came in for Petula's audition. Kathi had to practically drag Petula onto the stage, she was tugging at the leash so hard. It seemed that the only thing Petula wanted to do was bolt for the door.

"Come *on*, Petula," Kathi pleaded with the pig. "Just stand still onstage for a few minutes and you'll be done."

Kathi managed to drag the pig out to the middle of the stage. She unclipped the leash from Petula's collar and slowly backed away into the wings of the stage to watch Petula's audition.

"Face forward and smile, Petula," Kathi whispered. "Just like we practiced, remember?"

Petula stood still for about five seconds, and it looked to Darcy like she might stay there. But then she glanced over at Kathi and, without hesitating, dashed for the door.

"Noooooo!" Kathi cried, leaping toward the pig, catching her by the butt.

Darcy couldn't help but laugh. The sight of one of

her best friends diving after a pig and actually catching it was incredibly funny!

Ms. Harrington cleared her throat. "Um, Darcy, can you think of anything to help your friend?" She gestured toward Kathi, who now looked like she was wrestling with the pig.

Darcy felt her face flush. She hadn't meant to laugh at Kathi—it had just been too funny. Guiltily, she racked her brain for a solution. For some reason, Petula didn't want to stay on the stage. The lights had already been dimmed, so that couldn't be the problem.

What else do pigs care about? Darcy asked herself. She thought about her own pig, Orville. All Darcy ever saw him do was sleep, roll in the mud, and eat.

"That's it!" Darcy cried. Ms. Harrington and Kathi both jumped, startled. "Maybe Petula is just hungry, Kathi. Maybe that's why she doesn't want to stay on the stage. She's been waiting for her chance to audition for a few hours, so maybe she keeps bolting for the door because she's craving some delicious piggy treats, and she thinks she's more likely to find them outside than in here."

"You know, Darcy, I think you're right!" Kathi replied. "Petula usually eats a big mid-day snack right around this time, and I totally forgot to bring something with me to tide her over until dinner! I'm a terrible stage mom!"

Darcy put her arm around her friend. "Don't worry about it, Kathi. You were probably just as nervous about Petula's audition as she is. It's no wonder you forgot. Mack McCabe's farm isn't far from here. Jack and I can go over there to get a bucket of slop while some of the other animals audition. Then once she's had something to eat, she'll be ready to rock, so to speak."

"You'd do that, Darcy?" Kathi asked. "Thanks so much! You're the best friend in the world!"

Jack looked up at the two girls hugging. "Hey!" he cried. "What about me? I think I heard my name get volunteered in there, too. I think I deserve a hug, too."

He winked at Darcy.

"Dream on, Jack," Darcy said ruefully. "Now let's go get some slop."

Chapter 5

Wild Wisdom . . . *Squirrels rarely fall, but when they do they use their tails as parachutes to help slow their descent.*

The next morning, Darcy slept until after ten. The auditions the previous day had been so exhausting that she had needed some extra sleep. By the time she got downstairs, no one was in the kitchen having breakfast. Actually, it looked like all of the breakfast dishes had been cleared away long ago.

❋ ⟨ DARCY'S DISH ⟩ ❋

Man! This whole living-on-a-farm thing means you have to get up before the sun rises to get something to eat around here. In Malibu, the earliest you can get brunch is eleven. Here, if you get up at ten, you're three hours too late! And boy, could I have used a big plate of pancakes today! Yesterday's auditions didn't exactly turn out the way I planned. But the results come in today, so you never know. Catch ya later!

Darcy popped a few slices of bread in the toaster and rummaged around in the fridge for something else. By the time she had assembled a bowl of berries and yogurt, the toast was done. She spread some orange marmalade on it and slid it onto a plate. Then she arranged everything on a tray and took it outside.

"Good morning!" she called as she carried her tray into the garden. "Mom? Are you out here?"

"Over here!" Victoria called from the tomato patch. Darcy put her tray down on the table and headed over to the spot where her mom was kneeling in the dirt, mostly obscured by enormous tomato plants.

"Well, hello, sleepyhead," Victoria teased. "Decided to join us, have you?"

"Ha, ha, Mom," Darcy replied. "You have no idea how taxing those auditions yesterday were! I mean, they lasted for *hours*!"

"You're right, Darcy," her mom replied wryly. "I couldn't possibly know what it's like to spend sixteen hours a day on a movie set."

"Oh, um, right!" Darcy admitted sheepishly. "I'm so used to seeing you weeding and planting in the garden that I sometimes forget what you used to do all day long. Speaking of which—what *are* you doing in there?"

Victoria was standing in the middle of a patch of

tomato plants that had grown so high, they were almost as tall as Victoria herself.

"I'm just trying to pick some of these ripe tomatoes. I used a new organic fertilizer a few weeks ago, and ever since then, the tomatoes have gone crazy! The plants grew about two feet each in just two weeks, and there are so many tomatoes, I can hardly pick them fast enough! I'm having the same problem with the cucumbers. Eli's over there trying to wrestle a few of the ripe ones off the vine right now."

Oh, no! Darcy thought. *Eli in the garden is so not a good idea.*

Sure enough, she heard a loud yelp from Eli's general direction. Darcy rushed over to see if her friend was okay. She found Eli wincing in pain, his finger in his mouth.

"Nobody told me cucumbers have thorns!" Eli said accusingly. Darcy leaned over and twisted a cucumber off the vine.

"Huh," she said, looking closely at the vegetable. "You're right. But these aren't exactly huge thorns, Eli. I can scrape them off with my fingernail!"

She demonstrated for Eli, who turned a bright shade of crimson.

"Well, they're still prickly," he insisted.

"Okay, okay," Darcy shot back. "What are we going

to do with all of these tomatoes and cucumbers, anyway? There are way too many for us to eat. Actually, I think we could feed the entire town of Bailey for a week and *still* have tons of tomatoes!"

"Exactly!" Victoria chirped as she popped up behind Darcy.

"Uh, that's not exactly a good thing, Mom," Darcy pointed out. "We don't want the farm to smell like rotten veggies."

"Never fear, darling," Victoria soothed. "We'll think of something to do with all of this produce."

At that moment, an unexpected visitor arrived. Actually, make that two visitors. It was Jack, complete with a movie-director-style clipboard and bullhorn. Ms. Harrington trailed closely behind him, trying her best to keep up.

"Attention, ladies and gentleman!" Jack shouted into the bullhorn. "The results of the Bailey summer stock auditions are at hand!"

Ms. Harrington covered her ears. "Really, Jack," she scolded. "Is the megaphone necessary? I told you it was okay for you to come along, but you really must stop shouting into my ear. There are only three people here, and I'm sure the next town isn't really interested in the results."

Jack reluctantly lowered the megaphone, focusing instead on the clipboard. He cleared his throat and thrust his chest out officially.

"To begin, I am pleased to announce that Jack Adams has been cast as the voice of Wilbur, the pig."

He took a deep bow.

Victoria applauded enthusiastically, while Eli and Darcy joined in halfheartedly. "That's fantastic, Jack!" Victoria crowed. "Your father must be so proud of you!"

"Thank you," Jack replied. "It looks like my dreams of becoming a Hollywood star are about to become a reality."

The seriously intense look on Jack's face as he said this almost made Darcy giggle, but she stopped herself.

He ran down the rest of the cast, which included Petula as the actual Wilbur, Oprah as the lamb, Mini Me as Templeton the rat, and surprisingly, Kathi as the voice of Charlotte.

"Wow!" Darcy said, impressed. "I didn't even realize Kathi had auditioned."

"Well, actually, she didn't," Ms. Harrington replied. "Her voice was so commanding as she gave orders to Petula that I just thought she'd be a natural.

Plus, she'll have to be at all of the rehearsals with Petula anyway, so why not?"

"Makes sense," Darcy agreed. "What about me? I know I didn't actually audition, but do you think there's a role for me, Ms. Harrington?" Darcy asked eagerly. She couldn't bear the thought that Kathi was going to be in the play now, yet she didn't seem to have a role herself.

"Actually, I wanted to have a word with you about that, Darcy," Ms. Harrington said. "I have a very special and important role in mind for you, and I hope you'll accept it."

"Special and important?" Darcy's face lit up. "Do you mean like the narrator or the emcee? Oh, or maybe a co-director?"

"You're not too far off," Ms. Harrington said. "It's the role of animal wrangler."

"Really?" Darcy asked, her eyes wide with disbelief. "I like animals and everything, but Lindsay is much better with them than me. But that sounds like it could be cool."

Suddenly, it dawned on Darcy that she wasn't entirely clear on what an animal wrangler *was*.

"Oh, no!" she gasped. "Does that mean clean up after all of the animals or something?"

Before Ms. Harrington could reply, Victoria jumped in enthusiastically. "Not at all, Darcy," her mother explained. "The animal wrangler *is* like a director . . . a director for the animals! It's actually a very exciting job. There are a lot of them in Hollywood."

"Your mom's right," Jack said knowingly. "I know. I've studied everything there is to know about showbiz. Did you know that every single animal that appears in a TV show or a movie has to be specially trained while on the set?"

"You mean like Baron von Chimpie?" Darcy asked tentatively.

"Exactly!" Victoria agreed enthusiastically.

Victoria had starred in *Death Knocks at Midnight* with a chimp named Baron von Chimpie back when she had still been in the business. And Darcy and the rest of Bailey had been introduced to the baron when the Brennan brothers had temporarily adopted him as one of their exotic pets. The baron had been accustomed to show business, all right—he had been quite a diva!

Thinking about the baron automatically made Darcy think about his temporary guardians.

"But what about the Brennans?" Darcy asked. "Wouldn't they make much better animal wranglers than I would? I mean, they have a whole lifetime's experience working with exotic animals, and I only just started working at Creature Comforts this year."

"Actually, Darcy, I think you're just the right person for the job," Ms. Harrington said confidently. "The Brennans may have a lot of experience, but with their exotic animal business and their three-week trek through the Himalaya mountains this summer, I don't think they'll have much free time for the play."

"Well, thanks for the vote of confidence, but I don't know," Darcy said skeptically. "I mean, I like animals and all, but I'm not exactly a pro, even at Creature Comforts. Lindsay's always the one who knows what to do when an animal is sick, not me."

Ms. Harrington smiled. "But of course you know what to do around animals! Just think about how you figured out what was bothering Oprah and Petula yesterday. You have a real way with four-legged creatures, Darcy."

I do? Darcy thought. *Yes, I do!*

Darcy thought about all the animals she had worked with at the clinic since she had come to Bailey, and she realized that Kevin asked for her help just as much as he asked for Lindsay's.

"I guess you're right, Ms. H.," Darcy replied. "I *do* know animals. Take that squirrel over there."

Darcy pointed at a small brown creature nibbling on something in Victoria's garden.

"I'll bet I could train him to eat a nut right out of my hand!" Darcy boasted.

"Um, hate to break it to you, Darcy, but that's a chipmunk," Eli informed her.

Darcy's face fell. "Oh, right."

"Darcy, please accept the position," Ms. Harrington pleaded. "I have complete confidence in you. And there won't be any squirrels to train, so I think you'll do a wonderful job."

She smiled warmly at Darcy.

Oh, heck, Darcy thought. *What do I have to lose?*

"Okay, I've thought it over, and I would be happy to wrangle some animals," Darcy replied.

"It's settled, then," Ms. Harrington announced with a big smile. "Darcy will be the animal wrangler. Now there's just one last position for me to fill."

"Really?" Darcy asked. "What position is that?"

"I still need someone to help design and build the sets," Ms. Harrington said. "Do you know anyone who might be good at that?"

"Eli's pretty handy," Darcy said with a nod to her friend. "And if there are any squirrels on the set that need to be identified, there's someone to help me out."

"I think that's a wonderful idea," Victoria said. "Eli's a great help to have around, but this garden won't take up all of his time this summer."

"Well, Eli, what do you think?" Ms. Harrington asked.

"Sure," Eli agreed. "I like to build stuff."

"So you're good with a hammer, right?" Ms. H. asked.

"You bet!" Eli replied enthusiastically.

Darcy and Victoria exchanged a glance. *Uh-oh,* Darcy mouthed.

Chapter 6

Wild Wisdom . . . *Burmese pythons are one of the largest snake species—they can grow to weigh over two hundred pounds!*

The next morning, Darcy woke bright and early. It was going to be a long day—first Darcy had to work at Creature Comforts from ten to five, and then it was off to her first rehearsal.

She chose her outfit very carefully. If she was going to be a real animal wrangler, she had to dress the part. Not that she knew exactly what that meant, but she figured she had a good idea. If she was going to be working with animals, denim was key. But even though she was dressing like a cowgirl, that didn't mean she had to throw fashion to the wind.

"Ah, perfect!" Darcy cried, pulling out a totally cute pair of overalls. The denim fabric was covered in glittery embroidered flowers. Darcy paired the overalls with a lacy, flowery tank top and topped the whole outfit off with a sparkly pink cowgirl hat and cowboy boots.

Then she sat down at her laptop for a quick blog posting before she had to head off to Creature Comforts.

DARCY'S DISH

Okay, people, the verdict is in. I don't have an actual part in the play. Nope, my position is way cooler! You'll never believe it, but I, Darcy Fields, am the Bailey summer stock animal wrangler! That means I get to train the animals on the set, sort of like their acting teacher or director. Crazy, huh?

Watch out, Steve Irwin, Crocodile Hunter—here comes Darcy Fields—Animal Wrangler to the Stars!

"Ta-DA!" Darcy cried as she entered Creature Comforts. No one was there to greet her.

"Lindsay! Kevin!" she called out. "Where is everyone?"

"We're back here, Darcy," Kevin called from the back of the clinic.

Darcy entered the examining room, spinning around to show off her outfit.

"Well?" she asked. "How do I look?"

Lindsay looked up from the cat whose claws she had been clipping.

"Like a rock star dressed up as a cowgirl," Lindsay replied matter-of-factly.

"No, silly!" Darcy laughed. "I'm an animal wrangler!"

"A what?" Lindsay asked.

"An animal wrangler. I'll be training all of the animals in the cast of Bailey's summer stock production of *Charlotte's Web*."

"Wow, that sounds like a big job, Darce," her friend said. "Congratulations!"

"That's great news, Darcy," Kevin added. "I'm guessing that means you don't have much control over Jack, then, do you?"

"No, I don't," Darcy replied. "That would be Ms. H.'s thing."

Kevin sighed. "That's too bad," he said. "I'm afraid landing the role of 'voice of Wilbur' has caused Jack's ego to expand just a little."

"No!" Lindsay said dryly. "You could never accuse a kid like Jack of having an over-inflated ego."

Darcy giggled. "Well, I'll try to keep him in line if I can," she told Kevin seriously. "But I have a feeling I'll have my hands full with Wilbur the pig. And Oprah. And Mini Me. And all of the geese and goslings! Omigosh! What have I gotten myself into? This is a huge job for little old me, even if I am wearing this awesome hat."

Darcy sank into a chair and put her head in her hands. Lindsay sat down next to her friend and put her arm around Darcy's shoulders.

"Darcy, you're going to be great at this," Lindsay

said. "You're a natural with animals."

"Really?" Darcy looked up. She was surprised. She'd been told she was good at mixing and matching fashions, party planning, and even English class, but she'd never been told she was good with animals.

"Of course," Kevin added. "You've really learned quickly here at Creature Comforts, and animals always seem calmer when you're around."

"Wow, thanks, guys," Darcy said. "I guess I never realized that."

She felt pretty lucky to have such a supportive friend and an equally great boss.

The door chimes at the front of the shop rang.

"I'd better go see who that is," Kevin said.

"I can help," Darcy said as she followed Kevin to the door. It was the Brennan brothers, and between the two of them, they were holding the largest snake Darcy had ever seen.

"Wh-wh-wh-what *is* that thing?" Darcy asked as she moved back toward the examining room. She was seriously regretting that she had volunteered to help.

"This is a Burmese python," Brett answered. "Her name is Muffin."

"Muffin?" Darcy repeated incredulously. "She looks a little more like a 'Fangs' if you ask me!"

"Actually, Burmese pythons don't have fangs,"

Brandon chimed in. "They're constrictors."

"Is that supposed to make me feel better?" Darcy squeaked. "I mean, that thing could wrap itself around me and constrict me in no time!"

As Darcy continued to back away from the enormous snake, she noticed a large bulge about a third of the way down Muffin's body. She gasped.

"Oh, no!" Darcy cried, pointing to the bulge. "Does Muffin have a tumor?"

"Not at all," Brandon replied cheerily. "That's just Muffin's lunch. She ate a rabbit yesterday."

Darcy wrinkled her nose in disgust. "Ugh! That is so gross. How does she get an entire rabbit down? Her mouth is scary looking, but it doesn't look very big."

"It doesn't have to be very big," Kevin said simply. "Pythons have hinged jaws that open wide enough to swallow really large prey. Some pythons have been known to eat an entire pig."

"Yikes!" Darcy cried. "Kevin, you'd better keep Muffin away from Petula. Kathi said she was planning to bring her in today for a checkup, and Muffin definitely cannot eat her—she's the star of our summer stock show!"

"No need to worry, Darcy," Brandon reassured her. "Muffin here only eats about once a week, so that rabbit yesterday will keep her happy for a few more days to come. Kevin, I was hoping you could give her a quick checkup. You know how we like to bring her in once a year or so."

"Um, sure, no problem," Kevin replied. Darcy was pretty sure that he didn't look particularly thrilled, though.

"Darcy, I'll need some help in the back with this one," Kevin continued.

"You mean me?" Darcy squeaked, her voice sounding more scared than she would have liked. "I mean, what about Lindsay? She always helps you with the animals in the back."

"Actually, I have a package of medication that I'd like her to deliver to Hank Reading's farm, and I'm pretty certain Lindsay's the only one who knows how to get there," Kevin replied. "It's pretty far. And this will be a great chance for you to practice those wrangling skills!"

Darcy tried to put on a brave face.

"Future animal wrangler to the stars at your service!" she announced halfheartedly.

Meanwhile, back at the Fields' farm, Victoria was doing some wrangling of her own—with the cucumbers, that is.

"Oh, fiddlesticks!" Victoria cried. She was busy trying to figure out how to get out of the patch of garden where she was currently trapped by unruly cucumber vines.

Eli ran over from the tomato patch he was working in. "Everything okay?" he asked.

"Oh, yes, Eli," Victoria replied as she finally broke free from the vines. "I'm fine. I just had no idea cucumbers could get so *aggressive*."

She and Eli stared at the huge vines that had taken over much of the garden. The string beans and squash seemed to have been completely overrun with cucumbers. And on the other side of the garden, the tomato plants had grown so tall, they were blocking the pepper plants' sun.

Eli and Victoria had picked eight bushels of tomatoes and five bushels of cucumbers, and there were still tons more on the plants and vines.

"I don't know what you're going to do with all of these, Ms. Fields, but I hope it's something good!" Eli shook his head. "Because you sure do have a lot of them!"

Victoria wiped her brow and sighed. "Actually, Eli, I don't have a clue what one person does with all of this produce. I would love to give it away in town, but as Darcy said, I don't even think there are enough people in Bailey to eat all of this before it rots!

"I do know one thing, though," she continued. "Looking at all of these veggies is making me awfully hungry. What do you say we take a break from picking

63

and go inside for some lemonade and some turkey sandwiches . . . with tomato, of course!"

"Sounds good to me," Eli agreed, rubbing his stomach. "I'm famished."

Eli and Victoria entered the kitchen to find Jack already there, helping himself to the contents of the fridge.

Victoria cleared her throat. "Hello, Jack," she said, crossing her arms and giving him a stern look. "That's a delicious-looking sandwich you're making there."

"What, this?" Jack asked, referring to the triple-decker turkey, cheese, tomato, lettuce, and sprout sandwich he was about to bite into. "Aw, thanks!"

"I see my sarcasm is lost on you, Jack." Victoria chuckled. "Were you planning to offer me and Eli sandwiches as well, or were you just going to come in here, help yourself to the contents of my fridge, and then go on your merry way?"

Jack racked his brain for a second, as though trying to figure out which answer was the correct one. "Uh, the first one!" he mumbled through a mouthful of sandwich. "Definitely the first one. So, want a sandwich? I took everything out already."

Jack gestured to the kitchen counter, which was covered with jars of condiments, deli meats, and sandwich toppings.

"Yes, so I noticed," Victoria said as she pulled out

two pieces of bread and began to pile on turkey, ham, tomato slices, and cheese.

Jack continued to chow down on his enormous sandwich, pausing every once in a while to take a big bite of a crunchy dill pickle.

As Victoria listened to the steady crunching of Jack's pickle, she suddenly had a brilliant idea.

"That's it!" she cried, nearly causing Eli to drop the glass of lemonade he had just poured. "I've got it!"

"Got what?" Eli and Jack both asked in unison.

"I've figured out what to do with all of the tomatoes and cucumbers—pickles! I'll pickle the cucumbers and make tomato sauce. Then I can store the pickles and sauce in jars, and we'll be able to eat them for months and months to come."

"Cool," Eli said. "Have you pickled stuff before?"

"Well, now that you mention it, no, I haven't," Victoria replied. "But I don't see why I can't learn! With your help, I'm sure we'll figure it out."

"Awesome," Eli said. "I'm great in the kitchen, Mrs. Fields."

"I know you are, Eli," Victoria said confidently. "And I'm sure pickling is quite simple. This will be magnificent!"

Chapter 7

Wild Wisdom . . . *In just three years, a pair of rats is able to produce twenty million descendants.*

A few hours later, Eli and Victoria were up to their elbows in brine and vinegar solutions. Victoria had done some research and decided that they would make as many different types of pickles as they could. To her, the more pickles, the better!

In an effort to protect her clothing and get into the spirit of pickle making, Victoria had tied on an over-sized gingham apron. She was happily humming tunes from *The Sound of Music* as she tended the large pot of pickles on her half of the stove.

Eli's half of the stove was an entirely different story. Eli was wearing a ridiculous floral apron Victoria had procured for him, and the apron was now covered in splotches of vinegar, salt, and cucumber pieces. He also couldn't keep track of which recipe he was working on. Was this vat the salt brine solution or the vinegar solution? Eli stepped away from the stove to refer to the pages and pages of articles and websites that Victoria had printed out from the Internet. As he was shuffling through the papers, the vat that he had been tending began to bubble and boil over.

"Aw, man!" Eli shouted as he leapt to lower the jet. "This whole process makes me truly appreciate how easy it is to just buy a jar of pickles!" Eli shot Victoria a meaningful look.

"Oh, come on now, Eli," Victoria chided him. "Where's your sense of adventure? We're like pickle-producing pioneers!"

Eli responded by reaching for the jar of store-bought pickles Jack had been eating from earlier. He took out a pickle and took a loud, crunchy bite.

"Well, I may be a pickle-producing pioneer, but I sure do appreciate the delicious crunch of an assembly-line, factory-produced pickle," Eli said with a sigh.

Victoria snatched the rest of the pickle out of Eli's hand.

"You're only saying that because you've never tasted a homemade pickle," Victoria insisted. "My grand-mother used to make them all the time, and I must say, there's nothing like them in the world! Just wait and

see, Eli. In four to six weeks, we'll have dill pickles my
grandmother would have been proud of. And until then,
we've got some pickling to do!"

After a long day at Creature Comforts, Darcy headed
over to the playhouse for her first rehearsal. Though
she had been less than thrilled at the thought of holding
Muffin down while Kevin examined her, she had
managed to get through the experience unharmed. It
had certainly helped that the Brennans stuck around to
give Darcy a hand . . . Muffin was no lightweight! The
checkup had revealed that she weighed 175 pounds,
which was almost twice what Darcy weighed herself.
Yikes!

Darcy entered the theater to find that the rehearsal
was about to begin. Ms. Harrington was standing on
the stage distributing what looked like scripts, and the
animals and actors were all gathered around her. Ms.
Harrington saw Darcy enter and waved her over.

"Darcy! I'm so glad you're here," Ms. Harrington
said, relief in her voice. She picked up a large pile of
papers and handed them to Darcy.

"Should I distribute these to everyone?" Darcy
asked helpfully.

"Oh, no, dear," Ms. Harrington replied. "Those are
all for you."

Darcy's jaw dropped. "All of these?" she squeaked.
Darcy glanced around and noticed that all of the cast
members seemed to each be holding a very small stack
of papers. Hers was about five times the size of everyone else's.

"Why do I get so many more than everyone else?"
Darcy asked.

"Those are the stage directions for each individual
animal," Ms. Harrington replied. "So you have one
script for each animal character. But don't worry. You
won't have to memorize them. You can just refer to
them as we go."

She turned to face the cast members. "You, on the
other hand, will have to memorize your lines."

Kathi looked alarmed. "But I thought I was doing
a voice-over part. Doesn't that mean I'll be offstage the
whole time?"

"It does, but I'd still like all of the voice-overs
to memorize their parts eventually," Ms. Harrington
replied. "It will give you a better understanding of the
character if you don't have to worry about reading the
lines off a piece of paper."

"Oh, right!" Kathi said brightly, though Darcy
could tell she was terrified. "Memorization. That'll be
no problem." Then Kathi flipped through the script to
take a look at Charlotte's lines.

"Darcy!" she whispered to her friend. "Charlotte has a *lot* of lines in this play."

"Well, I'm guessing there's a reason it's called *CHARLOTTE'S Web*," Darcy whispered back. "She must have done lots of talking while she spun her webs! But don't worry. I'll help you practice your lines after rehearsal if you want."

"Really?" Kathi asked, sounding relieved. "You'd do that for me? Darcy, you're the greatest!"

Ms. Harrington clapped to get everyone's attention. "Okay, I'd like to begin. Let's have all of the animals over here." She pointed to the right side of the stage. "And let's have all of the people over on this side," she continued, gesturing toward the left side of the stage.

"Darcy, for now, why don't you lead the animals to their appropriate spots until they get used to being where they're supposed to be?" Ms. Harrington instructed.

"Sounds good, Ms. H.," Darcy replied. She flipped through the enormous stack of paper and pulled out the script labeled WILBUR. She scanned the first few lines and her hand shot up.

"Yes, Darcy," Ms. Harrington asked.

"It says here that in the beginning of the play, Wilbur is a tiny piglet that Fern has to cradle in her arms." Darcy looked at Petula and then looked at Lizzy, the ten-year-old girl who was playing the part of Fern. "I think Petula is bigger than Lizzy! There's no way she can cradle Petula in her arms without falling over."

"Excellent point, Darcy," Ms. Harrington said. "This is one of the occasions for which we will use a prop instead of an animal. I'll be sure to have the prop master find a stuffed pig toy that Lizzy can hold. Until today, we'll use this doll."

She handed a doll to Lizzy so that they could begin the opening scene, in which Fern saves piglet Wilbur's life. Darcy took Petula aside and tried to prepare her for her first scene. According to the script Darcy had been issued, most of Petula's time onstage would involve standing in a pen, but she did have to move from one side of the pen to the other pretty often. And sometimes she had to eat from a bucket that was supposed to contain slop.

She decided to practice getting Petula to move from one side of the pen to the other.

"Here, Petula!" Darcy called as she waved her arms over her head. The pig didn't budge.

Darcy tried to think of what types of things would get she herself to move from one side of a room to the other. Or from one side of a store to the other. *Fashion!* she thought. If she saw a totally adorable beaded purse on the other side of a store, she was sure to move toward it quickly. Could Petula have the same innate sense of fashion? Darcy figured it was worth a shot. She took off her sparkly pink cowgirl hat.

"Here, Petula!" she called, waving the hat in front of the pig. Petula actually swung her head back and forth, following the hat. *Wow,* Darcy thought. *This really works! Petula is one stylish pig!*

"Great job, Petula!" Darcy shouted encouragingly. *I really should have some sort of treats to give her,* Darcy thought. *Don't those sea lion trainers at the aquarium always have little fish for the sea lions after each trick they perform?*

Darcy whipped out a notebook and a fuzzy, sparkly pink pen. She jotted a note in bold letters at the top of the first page. It said: "Buy piggy treats." She didn't actually know what a piggy treat was, but she figured she could ask Kevin or Lindsay later. Darcy tucked the notebook back into her bag and swapped it for her PDA. Time to give her people a little update.

❋ ⟨ DARCY'S DISH ⟩ ❋

Well, it's true that there's no business like show business! Who could have imagined that I would spend my first rehearsal training a pig?! Next I have to train a ferret named Mini Me (don't ask) to pretend he's playing the part of a rat. All I can say is thank goodness there isn't an actual rat playing the role of the rat. That I totally could not handle!

"Okay, Layne," Darcy said reluctantly as she put her PDA away. "You and Mini Me are up next."

"Yeah, baby, yeah," Layne said as he sauntered onto the stage. Darcy took one look at him and gasped in horror.

Layne was dressed in a gray suit and was wearing a wig-type head covering that made him look bald, just like Dr. Evil. But worst of all, he had dressed poor Mini Me in an identical outfit, as though he really was Dr. Evil's tiny clone! Darcy was appalled. It was one thing for Layne to embarrass himself with his poor fashion choices, but it was a crime to subject that poor little ferret to the same fate. Where were the fashion police when you needed them?

"Layne, while those outfits are certainly *creative*, I'm afraid Templeton the rat would not be wearing a suit around the Zuckermans' farm," Darcy said. "Rats are supposed to be naked, and they definitely are *not* bald. I'm afraid if we want to be authentic, Mini Me is going to have to remove those clothes."

"No problem, no problem," Layne said smoothly.

"I'll remove the outfit if you give me—" He tucked his pinky into the corner of his mouth. "One *million* dollars."

Darcy rolled her eyes. "Layne, just take it off."

"All right!" Layne exclaimed as he started to unbutton his jacket.

"Not you! The ferret!" Darcy cried, panicking.

"Okay, okay," Layne said, scooping up Mini Me. He carefully removed the little suit and strange bald headpiece.

Once the ferret was appropriately naked, Darcy flipped open the script. She scanned it for Templeton's most difficult scene.

"Okay, it looks like the hardest thing Mini Me will have to do is roll a hard-boiled egg across the stage. Do you think he can do that?"

Layne shrugged. "I don't know. I've never tried to train him before."

"Well, I guess we'll find out," Darcy said. She flagged down the stage manager. "Do you think you have an egg-sized ball in your prop stash that I could borrow?"

Once the stage manager had produced the ball, Darcy placed it between Mini Me's front paws.

"Okay, Mini Me," she commanded. "Roll!"

The ferret sniffed the ball a bit but didn't budge. Darcy knelt down next to the ferret.

"Come on, Mini Me," she coaxed. "You can do it. Roll the ball!"

The ferret scurried over to Darcy and sniffed her shoes. Darcy sighed.

Maybe he needs a role model, she thought. *Like Dr. Evil!*

"Hey, Layne," Darcy asked. "Do you think you could help Mini Me out a bit?"

"Sure, anything for my little clone," Layne replied in a Dr. Evil accent. "What do you want me to do?"

Darcy flagged down the stage manager and got another ball.

"I think you should take this ball and model what we want Mini Me to do," Darcy explained. "Just pretend that you're Dr. Evil, rolling a ball across the stage on all fours, and that you want Mini Me to follow you. It'll be simple."

Layne narrowed his eyes at Darcy. "And you really think this will work? This isn't just some trick to get me to embarrass myself, is it?"

"Of course not!" Darcy was insulted. Why would she want to embarrass Layne? He was the one who dressed in a three-piece powder blue suit all on his own accord!

"I really think this might work," she continued. "I've seen baby ducks march in a line after their mother duck, so I don't see why it wouldn't work in this case."

"Okay, okay." Layne gave in. "Here goes nothing!"

Layne got down on all fours and batted the ball back and forth with his hands, rolling it along the stage.

"Come on, Mini Me," Layne said encouragingly. "You can do it!"

Mini Me continued to sniff around Darcy's feet, paying absolutely no attention to Layne. Darcy bent down and gently picked him up, turning him around so that he could see Layne.

"Roll, Mini Me, roll!" Darcy coaxed the ferret. "Follow Lay—I mean, Dr. Evil! You're his little ferret clone, so do what he does."

As soon as Darcy said "Dr. Evil," Mini Me perked up. He glanced over at Layne and saw him rolling the ball. Then, to Darcy's amazement, he followed Layne across the stage.

"Yes!" Darcy cried. "That's it, Mini Me! You're doing it! This animal wrangling thing is a piece of cake."

Chapter 8

Wild Wisdom . . . *Great horned owls have an opposable outer toe, which increases their ability to catch prey.*

The next day, Darcy was fast asleep, only it wasn't in her soft, fluffy purple-sheeted bed. It was on the counter at Creature Comforts. She had been sitting there diligently balancing the books for Kevin when her head had hit the counter.

"Cake . . . cake . . . German chocolate . . . piece of . . ." Darcy was mumbling in her sleep. Lindsay came up behind her friend and tapped her on the shoulder.

"Sleeping on the job, Darcy?" Lindsay asked.

"Cake!" Darcy cried as she jolted awake. "I'm not asleep! I'm balancing the books."

She gestured toward the papers in front of her, which were almost entirely untouched.

Lindsay gave Darcy a look, and Darcy sighed.

"I'm really sorry, Linds," Darcy said. "I'm just so

tired from yesterday's rehearsal. I had no idea training animals was so exhausting!"

"Yeah, you and Kathi have been pretty busy with the play lately," Lindsay noted. Darcy thought Lindsay sounded a little upset. But then Lindsay brightened.

"So, how's it going?" Lindsay asked chirpily as she hopped up on the counter next to Darcy.

"Actually, it went pretty well," Darcy replied. "Petula was great, once I discovered that we have something in common—a weakness for fine fashion! And Layne ended up being a real help with Mini Me. He actually got down on all fours and rolled a ball across the stage!"

"Wow." Lindsay shook her head, looking puzzled. "I can't say that I understand *any* of that, but it does sound like things went well, in a really weird way."

"Yup, they did," Darcy agreed. "Much better than I thought they would."

"Glad to hear it," Lindsay said. "Looks like we've got some customers."

An extremely tall man strode into Creature Comforts carrying a large cardboard box.

"Good morning," he greeted Lindsay and Darcy. "Is Kevin around?"

"Sure, he's in the back," Lindsay replied. "Can we help you with something?"

The man tipped the box so Darcy and Lindsay could see what was inside. It was the tiniest owl Darcy had ever seen.

"Aw," Darcy cooed. "It's the cutest! Is something wrong with it?"

"Well, I'm not sure," the man replied. "I found this baby great horned on the ground in my yard. I'm fairly certain it fell out of its nest, though I don't know what's wrong with it. It needs a more thorough examination."

"I'll go get my dad," Lindsay told the man. She reappeared a few seconds later with Kevin.

"Hello, Stewart." Kevin shook the man's hand vigorously. Then he peered into the box. "Looks like this little guy could use some help. Mind if I take a look?"

"Not at all," Stewart replied.

"Looks like a broken wing," Kevin said as he studied the tiny bird. "I know of a great raptor recovery center about a hundred miles from here that cares for injured owls and hawks and then releases them back into the wild. How about we send this guy over to them?"

"Sounds like a great idea, Kevin," Stewart replied. "I knew you'd have the answer."

"No problem," Kevin said warmly. "And there's no charge. Thanks for bringing him in. Lindsay and Darcy, do you think you can find a carrier for this owl? One that blocks out the light would be good. I'm sure it will

79

be a few days before the rescue center can schedule a pickup."

"If he's going to be sticking around for a while, we've got to give him a name," Darcy announced. "How about Mouse? You know, because he's so tiny?"

Kevin chuckled. "That's a little ironic, don't you think? Owls actually eat mice. It's one of their main food sources."

"Oh, right," Darcy said, recalling that she'd learned that in her fourth-grade science class. How had she forgotten? Some animal wrangler she was! Then inspiration hit her.

"I've got it!" she cried. "If he eats mice, why don't we call him Mousetrap? Then his nickname can be Mouse."

Lindsay and Kevin both laughed.

"I think that's the perfect name," Lindsay said. "Now do you think you can help me find a carrier for him?"

❊ (DARCY'S DISH) ❊

Whew! This whole working two jobs thing is rough. I'm exhausted already, and the day's only just begun. I've already named a baby owl (Mousetrap, if you must know) and helped him find a new home (well, in a pet carrier for now), and I'm off to another rehearsal. All of this work is seriously cutting into my blogging time, so sorry, folks! Catch ya later!

❊   ❊   ❊   ❊   ❊   ❊

When Darcy arrived at rehearsal, the first person she saw was Kathi, standing outside the playhouse looking miserable.

"Hey, Kathi." Darcy greeted her friend with a hug. She sure looked like she needed one!

"Hi, Darcy," Kathi replied glumly.

"What's wrong?" Darcy asked. "You look like someone just told you they've forever discontinued your fave brand of lip gloss!"

"I never should have agreed to this whole play thing!" Kathi cried. "Yesterday's rehearsal was a total disaster. I couldn't remember my lines, and then when I did, I couldn't get any of them out because I kept stuttering! Have you ever heard of a talking spider that stutters?"

"Well, no," Darcy replied. "But then again, I've never heard of a talking spider that spins magic webs, and isn't that what Charlotte is? Maybe a stutter will give her some extra character."

"Do you really think so?" Kathi asked hopefully.

"Sure, why not!" Darcy chirped. She was trying really hard to cheer Kathi up. "Or maybe you just need to practice more. I promised you I would help you with your lines, and I haven't forgotten. Plus, yesterday was only the first rehearsal. We still have weeks until the show, so you've got plenty of time to practice!"

Kathi smiled. "I guess you're right. I am being a little hard on myself. I mean, we did just start rehearsals. Jack was having trouble with his lines, too."

"That's the spirit!" Darcy said encouragingly. "And speaking of Jack, here comes the little squirt now."

Jack sauntered up to the girls. His baseball cap was on backward, he was wearing incredibly baggy pants, and he had a huge gold chain around his neck that had an enormous rhinestone-studded dollar sign hanging from it. Actually, Darcy was pretty sure that the chain was made of plastic and the dollar sign was coated in sequins, but the outfit did give Jack a certain look.

"Yo, yo, yo, ladies," Jack crooned to Darcy and Kathi. "How's it hangin'?"

"It's hanging just fine, Jack," Kathi answered, rolling her eyes.

"What's with the hip-hop gear?" Darcy wondered. "Last time I checked, you were playing Wilbur the pig in the play, not Snoop Dogg."

"Well, I've been thinking," Jack began. "*Charlotte's Web* is great and all, but this play is *old*. I did some research, and the book was written in the *fifties*. Do you have any idea how long ago that was? People wore poodle skirts and saddle shoes!"

"There's nothing wrong with poodle skirts!" Darcy interjected. Though she had winced at the words "saddle shoes," she adored her flouncy poodle skirt. She had to stick up for her fabulous skirt.

"Whatever," Jack said. "The point is, I thought this whole show could use an update. You know, something to bring it into the twenty-first century. So I thought hip-hop was the ticket. Want to hear some of my Wilbur the pig raps?"

"Wish I could, but I've got to head inside and start wrangling some animals!" Darcy said quickly as she ducked past Jack and into the playhouse.

"Yeah, me too!" Kathi added, hurrying after Darcy.

"Sheesh! Why is everyone so resistant to *change*?" Jack called after them. "It's called modernization of a classic! It's been done before, you know. Hello? Anyone ever heard of *Romeo and Juliet*?! They've redone that movie so many times, it's ridiculous!"

After rehearsal, Darcy and Kathi met up to walk home together.

"So, how'd it go today?" Darcy asked. "Any better?"

Kathi sighed. "I wish. I still couldn't stop stuttering. Ms. Harrington had a few tricks she tried teaching me, but none of them worked."

"What kind of tricks?" Darcy asked.

"Well, first I tried speaking more slowly, but I still couldn't get the words out. Then I tried a few different breathing exercises. Those worked a little bit, but mostly, they just made me out of breath!"

"Maybe practice is the trick," Darcy said. "If you want, come by Creature Comforts tomorrow before rehearsal. If things are slow, we can practice your lines. Maybe Lindsay can help, too!"

"That's really nice of you, Darcy," Kathi replied. "I'll totally be there. How did things go for you? Was Petula being good for you?"

"Petula's the best!" Darcy exclaimed. "She always knows where to stand, and whenever I wave something fashionable at her, she follows me wherever I want her to go. Today, for example, I just waved this sequined page boy cap at her, and she knew to follow it to her spot at the front of the barnyard!"

"Oh, yeah, that makes sense," Kathi said nonchalantly.

"It does?" Darcy was surprised. "Do you mean that all pigs have a penchant for fine fashion? I thought Petula and I had a special bond because we have the same taste!"

"No, silly." Kathi laughed. "Petula just really likes bright colors. You could probably wave a bright red pair of boxer shorts at her and she'd follow them, especially if you were leading her to a big bucket of slop."

Darcy laughed along with Kathi. Imagine her waving boxer shorts at Petula!

"Hey, did you hear about the costume scandal?" Kathi asked Darcy.

"Scandal?" Darcy's ears perked up. "What scandal?"

Kathi moved closer to Darcy as they walked.

"Well, I heard this from Samantha, who heard it from Emma, but apparently Ms. Harrington has no one to make the costumes for the play," Kathi confided.

Darcy looked puzzled. "That's a real bummer, but I don't see how that's scandalous."

"That's not the whole story," Kathi continued, her voice dropping to a whisper. "Ms. Harrington's cousin, Mildred Parker, has done the costumes for the Bailey summer stock show for years. You know Ms. Parker— she's the town historian. She's lived here her entire life, and she's been sewing the costumes ever since I can remember. Anyway, it turns out that all of a sudden, she decided to move. And you'll never believe where she moved to!"

"Okay, you've got me." Darcy shrugged. She had no idea where Bailey's resident historian/seamstress might want to relocate to. "Florida?"

"No!" Kathi cried. "Vegas! She's going to be a black-jack dealer! Isn't that crazy?!"

"Well, it's kind of unusual, but don't you think being the Bailey historian would get a little boring?" Darcy asked. "Maybe she just wanted a change of pace."

"I guess," Kathi conceded. "I just can't believe it. Poor Ms. Harrington! Who will she get to do the costumes?"

Darcy shrugged again. "I'm sure she'll find someone," she said. "After all, there are about a hundred people that live in this town, right? Someone else is bound to know how to sew."

"Very funny, Darcy," Kathi remarked. "There are at *least* a thousand people that live here. At *least*!"

Darcy put her arm around her friend. "I was only kidding, Kathi! I'll have you know that I've memorized the exact population posted on the 'Welcome to Bailey' sign on Main Street. Our population is precisely 1,678. People, that is. Livestock is a whole different story."

"Ha, HA!" Kathi said triumphantly. "I knew it! Small town? No way!"

Darcy gave Kathi a look.

"Okay, okay," Kathi conceded. "It is a small town. But you've got to admit you love it here, Darcy. Come on, I know you do."

Darcy sighed. "I can't even believe I'm going to admit this, but you're right. There's no place like home, and for me, home is the crazy town of Bailey!"

Chapter 9

The kitchen was a total mess. After a few days spent making bread-and-butter and dill pickles, Victoria had announced that it was time to move on to the tomatoes. The task of the day was to cook up enormous vats of tomato sauce and chop up tomatoes for a spicy salsa recipe Victoria had created. Eli was proudly wearing a clean apron, and this one had bright pink ruffles and flowers all over it.

"I think it's quite a nice look for you, Eli," Victoria said.

Suddenly, a huge flash lit up the kitchen.

"What the heck?" Eli cried as a few more flashes were aimed in his direction.

A second later, Jack was standing in the middle of the kitchen, a large camera slung around his neck.

"That is definitely a great look, Eli," Jack agreed.

"And now I've captured it on film for the rest of Bailey to see. For a small fee, of course."

Jack winked at Victoria, who glared back at him, holding out her hand.

"Hand that camera over instantly," she scolded.

"Aw, come on," Jack whined. "This is an incredible moneymaking opportunity! I'll share the proceeds with Eli. Say, a ninety-ten split. *And* I'll donate that ten percent to your favorite charity. Come on, Eli. What do you say?"

"Jack," Victoria warned. "The camera, please."

Jack reluctantly handed over the camera, which Victoria promptly opened and emptied. Then she handed it back to Jack, who immediately loaded a new roll of film.

"Don't even think about taking more photos of Eli, Jack!" Victoria cried, reaching for the camera again.

"Don't worry," Jack said smoothly. "I'm really only interested in snapping a shot of Victoria Fields hard at work making pickles and tomato sauce for the upcoming winter in Bailey."

"And are these photos ones you're planning to sell to the highest-bidding tabloid newspaper?" Victoria asked shrewdly.

"Of course not!" Jack replied. "I can't even believe you would suggest such a thing! These photos are for the *Bailey Daily News*'s upcoming cooking issue. I thought you'd be flattered to be featured."

Victoria's skepticism faded. "Of course I am, Jack," she said. "It's very sweet of you to think of me. Now, I'll pose for two photos, on the condition that this is an exclusive story for the Bailey Daily News only. These photos are not, under any circumstances, to appear in any other magazine, newspaper, or tabloid or on any TV news show or website. Agreed?"

Jack stuck out his hand. "Deal," he said, and the two shook on it.

"Now, where should I stand?" Victoria asked.

"Why don't you stand right there, near the pot of sauce on the stove?" Jack asked.

Victoria positioned herself in front of the stove, raising a wooden spoon as a prop.

"Perfect!" Jack crowed as he snapped a photo. "Excellent! That's it. Looking good. Just turn a little to the left. Fantastic!"

Jack quickly snapped at least ten photos.

Blinded by the flash, Victoria groped for the cookbook. "Okay, that's enough, Jack," she said. "It's time for Eli and me to get back to work. Unless, of course, you'd like to help?" She raised her eyebrows at him.

"Uh, no, thanks," Jack blurted as he backed out of the kitchen. "I've got to go, uh, work on this article for the paper before rehearsal this afternoon. Yeah, that's right. Gotta run!"

In a flash, he was out the door.

Eli shook his head. "Crazy kid," he muttered as he stirred a pot of sauce on the stove. "And speaking of getting back to work, do you think I can take a little break? My arm is really aching from all this stirring. I feel like I've been stirring for hours, and I think I may be getting carpal tunnel syndrome!"

"Well, we can't have that now, can we?" Victoria chirped. "I'd be happy to stir for a while. In the meantime, why don't you chop up this bushel of tomatoes for the salsa? Then you'll have to chop up this bushel of onions and this pile of cilantro. Then mix them all together with some vinegar, lemon, and spices for a delicious salsa. Easy peasy!"

"Thanks, I guess," Eli said. He sank into a chair and started chopping. Once he had finished all of the tomatoes, he moved on to the onions. Within a few seconds, though, tears were streaming down his face. Victoria heard him sniffling and turned to see his red, swollen eyes.

"Oh my goodness, Eli, what is it?" she shrieked. "Did you cut yourself?" She rushed over to Eli, who was wiping his eyes on the flowered apron.

"No, it's these onions!" Eli said as he blinked to try to stop crying.

At that moment, Darcy entered the kitchen, her nose buried in a library book. She plunked herself down at the table and put down the book, revealing that she, too, had been crying!

"Not you, too!" Victoria cried, rushing over to Darcy. "What is it? It can't be the onions—they're all the way over there!"

"Onions?" Darcy asked, confused. "What onions? I'm crying because I just got to the end of *Charlotte's Web*. I'm reading it again because I thought it would be a good refresher for the play. And I can't believe how tragic it is! This is no children's book!"

Darcy pushed the book aside in disgust. Then she buried her head in her hands, sobbing.

"Darcy, dear," Victoria said as she patted her daughter on the back. "Did you ever consider that perhaps that's the best kind of book for children . . . one that tells the truth? It may be sad, but it's simply a realistic portrayal of life."

Darcy lifted her head from the table. "Huh," she said thoughtfully. "I hadn't thought of it that way." She wiped her eyes. "Thanks for that insight, Mom."

Then Darcy glanced over at Eli, who still had tears

streaming down his face as he chopped the onions.

"Didn't you hear what my mom said, Eli?" Darcy asked him. "There's no reason to cry at the end of *Charlotte's Web*—it's real life. You know, tough love. That kind of thing."

"Um, yeah," Eli affirmed. "But I'm not crying about the book. It's the onions!"

"Well, it's time to leave the onions behind because we've got a rehearsal to get to! Mom, I have to take Eli with me today. Ms. Harrington specifically asked me to bring him along so that he can help with the sets today."

"Of course!" Victoria said. "Eli, we can finish the salsa and sauce tomorrow. It should be our last day of cooking for a while. Hurrah!"

Eli quickly shed the apron and headed out the door after Darcy.

"Sounds great!" he called over his shoulder. "See you tomorrow!"

By the time Darcy and Eli arrived at the playhouse, rehearsal was in full swing. On one side of the stage, Kathi was stuttering out a few lines opposite Jack, who was furiously writing in what looked like a reporter's notebook between takes. On the other side of the stage, Darcy saw Layne and Mini Me rolling balls back and forth to each other.

"Eli! Darcy!" Ms. Harrington rushed over to them as soon as she spotted them. "Perfect timing. Eli, I'm hoping you can help RJ with the barn door. She's been quite helpful, but I'm afraid she keeps scaring off everyone I send over there to assist her."

Eli gasped. RJ was the trapper's daughter, and she was pretty tough. In fact, she could be downright ornery.

At that moment, Eli and Darcy overheard RJ's voice coming from backstage.

"What's the matter? Cat got your tongue? Fer cryin' out loud, I asked how those boards came to be nailed on all crooked like that?!"

A second later, a girl Darcy assumed had been responsible for the crooked board ran out from backstage in tears and headed straight for the door.

Ms. Harrington sighed. "See what I mean? Eli, I know you can handle RJ—we all know her bark is a lot worse than her bite."

Eli didn't look so sure.

"Yeah, sure, Ms. H.," he said bravely. "I can handle it."

Darcy backed away slowly. "And I'll just head over to the animals!" she said quickly.

"Not so fast, Darcy," Ms. Harrington said. "I'm hoping you can give Eli a hand for a bit. We're pretty far behind with the sets, and RJ and Eli could really use your help."

"Me?" Darcy asked. "But don't I need to go work with the animals?"

"Yes, of course," Ms. Harrington replied. "But you've been doing such a great job with them that I think they can have a day off. And another set of hands on the sets would really help things. Would you mind, Darcy?"

"Sure, no problem," Darcy said, following Eli toward the stage. "Those cuddly critters deserve a break. And in the meantime, Eli and I can totally handle this set thing."

❋ DARCY'S DISH ❋

Remember RJ? The surly trapper's daughter I've mentioned before? Well, it turns out Eli and I have been assigned to help her with—you won't believe this—set building! Not only do I have to use a hammer (and I just polished my nails in pretty plum last night!), but I also have to be near Eli while he wields one. Wish me luck—I'm definitely going to need it!

❋   ❋   ❋   ❋   ❋   ❋

Eli and Darcy approached RJ tentatively. She was busy hammering boards together, a fierce look on her face as she slammed the hammer onto each nail. Eli opened his mouth to say something, but Darcy grabbed his arm just before he got the words out.

"Wait!" Darcy whispered, pulling Eli back. RJ continued slamming the nails as if her life depended on it. "Let's butter her up a little before we tell her we're helping out," Darcy suggested. "You know, offer her something. I've got a cold orange juice in my bag, and she sure does look thirsty."

Eli considered the orange juice Darcy had just pulled out of her bag. It *did* seem like an icebreaker was worth a shot. He took the orange juice and stepped toward RJ.

"Hey, RJ," Eli said, keeping his distance.

RJ lifted her head. "What are you lookin' at?" she snapped.

"I just thought you might like some juice," Eli offered. "You look like you might be thirsty, seeing as you're working so hard there."

"Good one!" Darcy whispered as she nudged Eli in his side. Darcy smiled sweetly at RJ, who looked from Eli to Darcy suspiciously. Then her face softened and she reached for the juice.

"Aw, shucks," RJ said. "That's awful thoughtful

of you." She slugged down most of the juice and then picked up her hammer.

"Ms. Harrington said you might need some help," Darcy said. "Can Eli and I do something?"

RJ still looked suspicious, but she nodded.

"Suit yourselves, greenhorns," she said, handing Eli a hammer and some nails. "The door of the barn needs some work. Just hammer those planks together, then mount the door on those hinges there."

Then she handed Darcy a bucket of paint and a paintbrush.

"And you can paint that picket fence white," she told Darcy. "That is, if you think you can handle it, tenderfoot."

Darcy grabbed the paint and brush. "Aye, aye, Captain," she said, giving RJ a salute. She was shocked to see RJ crack a smile.

"Captain!" RJ said thoughtfully. "I like that."

Then the scowl returned. "Now get to work!" she barked.

Eli picked up his hammer and consulted the pile of boards in front of him. Then he selected a thin piece and began nailing it into what was supposed to be the barn. He was surprised to find that it wasn't as hard as he thought it would be.

"Hey, this is pretty simple!" Eli shouted with excitement.

"Back to work!" RJ barked. "Ain't no time for celebrating until the job's done, greenhorn. Keep nailin' in those boards until we have ourselves a door!"

"Okay, okay," Eli mumbled. "Sorry, *Captain*."

Meanwhile, Darcy was daintily coating the fence with paint. Since the last things she had painted were her fingers and toenails, she pretended she was giving the fence a mani and pedi. Well, a rather dull *white* mani and pedi, but whatever!

She treated each individual board as though it was a fingernail, and she was very careful to paint each one without any splashing.

RJ glanced over and saw Darcy delicately dipping the paintbrush into the can of paint. Grumbling, she strode over to Darcy and grabbed the brush out of Darcy's hand.

"Fer cryin' out loud!" RJ shouted. "Stop being so namby-pamby. You've got to put some effort into it and slap that paint on. You don't have to be so dainty."

"Um, okay," Darcy said as she watched RJ demonstrate by aggressively slathering paint all over the fence. Darcy took back the paintbrush and thrust it into the paint can.

"Well, here goes!" she said as she haphazardly slapped a brush full of paint on. "This is actually kind of fu—"

As she sloshed the paint onto the fence, it splashed all over the leg of her jeans. It was a fashion disaster! Her fabulous boot-cut Seven jeans had white paint splattered all over them!

"Ack!" Darcy cried. "I got paint all over me! My jeans are totally ruined."

"Ain't no big deal," RJ scoffed. "Clothes are meant for gettin' dirty."

"Not these clothes!" Darcy explained. "These are my favorite jeans." Then suddenly, inspiration struck her.

"RJ, do we have any other paints?" Darcy asked. "You know, in colors other than white?"

"Yeah," RJ replied. "There should be some red, pink, and turquoise in back."

"Perfect!" Darcy leapt up and dashed off to find the paint. When she returned, she had expertly splashed her jeans in a rainbow of colors. They looked fantastic!

Darcy noticed RJ looking at the jeans approvingly in spite of herself. "Not bad," RJ grumbled. "Now—"

"I know, I know," Darcy finished with a smile. "Back to work!"

A few hours later, Darcy's picket fence was pure white and Eli was just hammering the last board on to form the barn door. Darcy prepared herself to make a big entrance onstage to test Eli's door and show off his expert craftsmanship.

"Ready, Eli?" Darcy called from what was supposed to be the inside of the barn. Eli was waiting on the other side of the door, his fingers crossed that the door wouldn't fall off the hinges when Darcy swung it open.

"As ready as I'll ever be!" Eli replied. "Go for it!"

RJ stood back to watch as Darcy strode toward the door, flinging it open. Much to everyone's surprise, though, the door didn't budge. Darcy rattled the doorknob a few times. Then she noticed that the nails that were holding the planks of the door together were also holding the door shut in its frame. Eli had hammered the door to the frame, and there was no way it was opening without some major reconstruction!

"Uh, Eli?" Darcy asked. "Did you hammer the boards together *before* you put the door on? Or did you hammer the boards *to* the door frame?"

"Aw, man!" Eli cried. "I must be cursed! How was I supposed to know you had to nail the boards together first?"

Darcy just shook her head. Some things never changed!

Chapter 10

Wild Wisdom . . . *The best time to take a puppy away from its litter and to its new home is when the puppy is forty-nine days old.*

The next day, Darcy swooped into Creature Comforts, proudly sporting her paint-splattered jeans.

"Good morning!" she crowed. "It's a beautiful day, isn't it?"

"Well, someone sure is chipper this morning," Lindsay remarked as she drew a checkmark on her clipboard. She was in the middle of doing the clinic's weekly inventory.

"It must be my new look!" Darcy explained, modeling her jeans for her friend.

"Nice!" Lindsay said approvingly. "What happened, you splashed paint on them and had to cover it up?"

"How'd you guess?" Darcy gasped. She had no idea her friend knew her so well!

"Well, it's a pretty obvious trick," Lindsay replied sagely. "I've done it before myself, only it was on a denim jacket."

"Oh, that sounds totally cute!" Darcy said as she leaned against the counter. "You should wear it more. So, what are we working on today? Inventory?"

Lindsay sat down at the counter. "Yup, inventory," she said with a sigh.

Darcy was surprised. It wasn't like Lindsay to be so unenthusiastic about inventory day. Lindsay was usually moving a mile a minute on Wednesdays, checking things off of lists on her clipboard, counting bottles of vitamins, and stacking shelves with cans of dog food.

"Is everything okay, Lindsay?" Darcy asked. "You seem a little down."

"What? Me?" Lindsay replied, brightening a little. "Oh, I'm fine."

"Well, okay. Where should I start?" Darcy asked. "Do you want me to stack these doggie biscuits on that shelf right above Snoozie?"

"Yeah, sure," Lindsay said, but Darcy thought she still seemed distracted. If something really was bothering Lindsay, Darcy knew of one way to help her friend open up—she would make her laugh!

"Speaking of doggie biscuits," Darcy said, "I thought of a totally cool display for the window last night. What if we came up with a themed display to attract more customers? We can hang some doggie biscuits from the ceiling with some fishing line—you know, so you can't see the strings. Then we can use some cotton batting and hang it from the ceiling so it looks like it's suspended, too. Then, as the final touch, we can make wings for some of the abandoned puppies Mr. Anderson brought in last week, and we can hang *them* from the ceiling, too!"

Darcy paused for effect. "I'll call it 'Doggie Heaven'!"

Lindsay barely batted an eyelash. "Yeah, sure," she replied. "Great idea."

Darcy couldn't believe her ears. She strode over to her friend, placing her hand against Lindsay's forehead.

"Hello? Earth to Lindsay Adams!" Darcy called. "Are you feeling okay? I just suggested hanging puppies from the ceiling with fishing line so that they look like doggie angels, and you didn't even crack a smile! What's going on?"

Lindsay seemed to snap out of her reverie. "Oh! Sorry, Darcy," she apologized. "I've just been a little distracted. What did you say about a doggie heaven?"

"Well, I thought the dangling doggie treats and clouds could be a fun window display, but I was just joking about using the puppies as props," Darcy explained. "Come on, Lindsay. Something must be bothering you. What is it?"

Lindsay leaned on the counter, her chin in her hands. "Well, to be honest, I've been feeling a little bored," she admitted. "I don't know what's wrong with me! I usually love working here in the summers, but this year it's different. I mean, you and Kathi are running off to play rehearsals all the time, and even Jack is busy practicing his lines and working on some sort of 'new business venture' he keeps hinting at."

Lindsay looked like a sad, lost puppy. Darcy hadn't meant to make Lindsay feel left out, and she felt like a terrible friend.

"I've been totally insensitive, Lindsay," Darcy apologized. "I've been talking about the play nonstop, and I never even stopped to consider how that might make you feel."

Lindsay sighed. "It's not your fault, Darcy," she said. "I just need to find a hobby to keep me busy this summer when I'm not at work."

"A hobby! Omigosh. I can totally help you pick one! What were you thinking of?" Darcy asked. "You could take up tap dancing. Or yoga. Or you could start writing a journal. And there are always crafts. Knitting is supposed to be really cool and hip, and lots of young people are learning how to do it. Or you could try scrapbooking or—"

Darcy paused. Lindsay was trying hard not to laugh.

"What?" Darcy asked. "What's so funny? Oh! You want to try comedy. Yeah, that would be cool. You'd be a good comedian!"

"No!" Lindsay cried. "Darcy, I was laughing because of how you totally launched into ten thousand different things I could do with my free time. I appreciate your enthusiasm, but I do have a few thoughts of my own, you know."

"Right," Darcy said sheepishly. "Sorry. I just had so many ideas—"

Darcy gasped, covering her mouth with her hands.

"Oh. My. Gosh," Darcy continued. "I totally just thought of another completely perfect idea, but now I can't tell you because I don't want to interfere with your independence!"

Lindsay considered her friend for a moment. "You might as well tell me and then let me decide," Lindsay cajoled Darcy. "Come on, spill!"

"Okay!" Darcy gushed. "You can be the seamstress for the play! I know you like to sew, and you obviously have a great sense of fashion. I mean, you had the same idea as I did about paint-splattered denim. And I know Ms. Harrington needs someone to design and make the costumes, and I can totally help you out. So, what do you say?"

"That does sound like fun," Lindsay agreed. "But

Ms. Parker always does all of the costumes. She's so good at it. Why can't she do the costumes this year?"

"Didn't Kathi fill you in?" Darcy asked. "Ms. Parker flew the coop! She decided she'd had enough of Bailey, and she headed for Vegas to become a blackjack dealer. So there's no one to make the costumes—except you, of course!"

Lindsay thought about it for a moment.

"Well, it would be fun to be involved in the play," Lindsay conceded. "I guess if Ms. Harrington really needs my help, I can't say no."

"Yes!" Darcy shrieked. She jumped up and threw her arms around Lindsay. "This will be so much fun!"

Suddenly, Kevin poked his head out from the back of the clinic.

"What on earth is going on out there?" Kevin asked. "I never knew inventory day could be so exciting."

"Sorry, Dad," Lindsay said sheepishly, glancing at Darcy. "We're not being very professional, are we?"

Kevin looked from one girl to the other. He put his hands on his hips and pretended to look stern, but Darcy and Lindsay could both tell he was only joking around. Darcy always thought it was funny that Lindsay's dad could be such a big goofball.

"Well, who's going to tell me what this is all about?" Kevin asked.

Darcy shrugged. "I think it should be Lindsay."

"Dad, Darcy just asked me if I would consider designing the costumes for *Charlotte's Web*," Lindsay told her father calmly, trying not to sound too excited. "And I was kind of hoping that you would say it was okay. I probably won't be able to work here at Creature Comforts quite as much, but I'll still come in to help out whenever I can. I promise!"

"That certainly sounds exciting," Kevin said. "You're a very creative young lady, Lindsay, and I think it's a good idea to put some of that creative energy to use from time to time. You always were artistic, even as a little girl."

Kevin's face took on a dreamy look, as though he was thinking about something in the past. Lindsay caught Darcy's eye, and the two girls both cringed. Kevin was obviously about to embark on one of his infamous trips down memory lane.

"I remember one time when you were about four or five," Kevin said to Lindsay. "I had made orange-and-cherry Jell-O for dessert. You weren't interested in eating it, but you were *very* interested in turning it into a sculpture and then in using it as finger paint to decorate the wall behind you."

Kevin chuckled at the recollection, and then he

became serious, wagging his finger at his daughter. "Not that I was happy about that mural!"

"Sorry?" Lindsay ventured. "It was a long time ago, Dad. And I promise you that I will never again create a mural using Jell-O."

Kevin gave Lindsay a hug. "That's my girl," he said warmly. "Now, why don't you two go take a long lunch break? I'm sure you have some costume planning to do, and you can finish up the inventory when you get back."

"Really?" Lindsay asked, a smile lighting up her face. "Thanks, Dad!"

"Yeah, thanks, Kevin," Darcy added. "Let's go!"

Darcy grabbed Lindsay's hand and pulled her out the door.

Ten minutes later, Darcy and Lindsay were seated at the Bailey Hometown Diner. Darcy was happily munching on a veggie burger and fries, while Lindsay was digging into an enormous Cobb salad. A chocolate milk shake with two straws sat in the middle of the table.

Darcy pulled a hot-pink notebook and a funky plaid-print pencil case out of her bag. She opened the notebook and selected her favorite pencil—a purple one with sparkly purple feathers at the end instead of an eraser.

"First, you'll have to come up with some designs for the different costumes," Darcy instructed as she pushed the pencil and notebook across the table toward Lindsay. "Then we'll have to go shopping for materials."

"Okay," Lindsay said as she picked up the pencil and began to sketch. "I thought Wilbur might like a tux. You know, something to make him feel special when he's hanging out all day in his smelly pigpen."

Darcy laughed as she watched Lindsay quickly sketch a chubby pig in a tuxedo.

"Ha, ha," Darcy said. "The costumes are for the *people*, Lindsay, not the livestock. They already have costumes—their birthday suits!"

"No!" Lindsay gasped in mock disbelief. "You're not going to make them go onstage—" Lindsay lowered her voice to a whisper. "Naked?"

Darcy and Lindsay both broke into giggles. Darcy wasn't sure what was funnier—the idea of a pig in a tuxedo or the thought that all the animals would technically be naked onstage.

"Okay, okay," Lindsay said, pulling herself together. "I'm ready to sketch for real now."

As Lindsay quickly sketched a few outfits, Darcy typed a quick blog posting on her PDA.

DARCY'S DISH

Okay, quick update. I'm here at the Bailey Hometown Diner with Lindsay for lunch. (Side note: they have the BEST fries, ever—even better than the ones at Rick's Drive-in in Pasadena!) Anyway, guess what? Lindsay just agreed to design costumes for the play. And let me tell you, that girl can sew! She's busy sketching designs as I write. And as the one who suggested that she join the crew, I get to be her special costume design consultant. Cynthia Rowley print button-down shirts with overalls, here we come! Lindsay and I are going to bring some new fashions to the farm. Toodles!

"What do you think of these two outfits for Fern?" Lindsay asked as she slid the notebook across the table to show Darcy.

Darcy glanced at the drawings. The first sketch was a cute plaid-print dress with a rounded collar. The second drawing was of a classic pair of overalls paired with a cap-sleeved button-down shirt in a pretty floral print.

Darcy was impressed. She knew Lindsay could sew, but who knew she could come up with such perfect designs so quickly!

"Lindsay, these rock!" Darcy complimented her friend. "We can check out the thrift store for overalls, jeans, and other basic items, and then we can pick out prints at the fabric store for the shirts and dresses."

"Great idea!" Lindsay agreed as she leaned over to steal the last french fry off Darcy's plate. "I'll work on sketching out all of the designs today after work, and then maybe we can go shopping after you get out of rehearsal."

"Sounds good," Darcy agreed. Then she glanced down at her plate.

"Hey!" she cried, crossing her arms and pouting. "That was my last fry!"

"Consider it a favor," Lindsay said as she glanced at her watch. "I was just helping you finish. Come on, we've got to get back to Creature Comforts to finish the inventory."

Chapter 11

Wild Wisdom . . . *Alligators have approximately eighty teeth in their mouth at one time. When the teeth wear down, they are replaced. Consequently, an alligator can go through two to three thousand teeth in its lifetime.*

When Darcy and Lindsay entered Creature Comforts, they were in for a big surprise. Kevin was casually sitting on a chair in the middle of the room, a five-foot-long alligator at his side!

"Oh, hello, girls," Kevin greeted them. "Have a nice lunch?"

Lindsay and Darcy backed away from Kevin and the alligator, and Darcy fumbled behind her for the doorknob.

"D-D-Dad?" Lindsay whispered, her eyes wide with fear. "You're sitting next to an alligator!"

"Actually, that statement is incorrect," Kevin said pleasantly. "This is a caiman, which looks like an alligator but is a bit different. Caimans are smaller than alligators, and they're found in Central and South America. Alligators, on the other hand, are native to the southeastern United States and eastern China."

"And why exactly is there a caiman in the middle of Creature Comforts?" Lindsay asked.

"Oh, that's easy!" Kevin said. "I'm keeping an eye on him while the Brennans prepare their truck so that they can get him to the reptile house at the San Diego Zoo."

Kevin seemed to sense that Darcy and Lindsay weren't pleased with the caiman's presence. Suddenly, something dawned on him, and he chuckled. "Don't worry, girls," he told them. "Carl here has been tranquilized, and he's not a threat to any of us."

"Carl?" Darcy giggled. "That's a strange name for an enormous lizard, don't you think?"

"Well, the previous owner named him. A man who owns a farm about fifty miles from here thought it would be fun to have one of these as a pet. So, he imported Carl all the way from South America when he was a tiny baby. But as Carl kept growing, the man realized that he couldn't handle such a huge reptile as a pet. He was afraid Carl would eat some of his livestock!"

"Wow!" Lindsay said. "That's crazy. Is Carl fully grown now, or will he still get bigger?"

"Caimans can grow to be sixteen feet long, so he may

still grow quite a bit," Kevin replied. "That's why the Brennans are taking him to San Diego. The only safe place for a creature like this is out in the wild or at the zoo, not on a farm!"

"I'll say," Lindsay said, still eyeing Carl warily. "So, should we finish doing inventory and just work around Carl as we go?"

"Sounds good to me," Kevin said cheerily. "Carl and I will just hang out over here, out of the way."

Suddenly, Lindsay noticed that Kevin had a large syringe partially concealed in his left hand.

"Uh, Dad?" Lindsay asked. "If Carl's so tranquilized and harmless right now, why are you sitting there next to him trying to hide that enormous syringe?"

"Oh, this," Kevin said with a nervous laugh. "Well, Carl certainly is out cold, but the Brennans wanted me to keep an eye on him, just in case. If the tranquilizer starts to wear off a bit and Carl starts to stir, I'm supposed to hit him with this, pronto." Kevin held up the syringe, which was about five times the size of the syringes he normally used.

"Ahhh!" Darcy shrieked. "That syringe looks like something out of a horror movie. Actually, my mom did one of those once. It was called *Possessed Puppy: Man's Best Friend*, and it was about a crazed little puppy that goes after the owner and her kids. There's this crazy scene where my mom wields a syringe full of puppy tranquilizer just like that one." Darcy shuddered. "Even though it's my mom and I know it's just a movie, that scene still gives me shivers."

"Well, don't worry, girls," Kevin said confidently. "You're in good hands here. And Carl's not about to star in any animal horror movies, so hopefully I won't have to use this syringe!"

Darcy and Lindsay moved around the clinic, gingerly stepping over Carl when necessary. Darcy filled up the shelf above Snoozie with doggie biscuits. Then she moved on to counting the number of leashes hanging on the rack behind the register. They had sold four that week alone, so Darcy went into the back room to find four new leashes to replace the ones that had been sold.

Finally, inventory was done. Carl was still slumbering peacefully on the floor, and Lindsay noticed that Kevin was also dozing and slipping down a bit in his chair.

"Dad!" Lindsay said sharply.

"What?!" Kevin cried, leaping out of his chair, his syringe at the ready.

Lindsay put up her hands as though she was being arrested. "Whoa, Dad," she said soothingly. "Lower the syringe."

Kevin looked at the syringe in his hand sheepishly. "Oh, sorry, sweetie," he apologized.

"Dad, you're not supposed to doze off when you're in charge of watching over a five-foot-long sedated caiman named Carl!" Lindsay scolded her father.

Kevin yawned. "You're right, honey," he said sleepily. "I was up at four this morning to see Vince McMann's new foal, and I guess I'm just feeling a little sleepy. Tell you what. You wouldn't mind standing guard over Carl here until the Brennans get back, would you? They should be here any minute now—they just had to load up the truck with supplies for the trip and create some sort of pen to hold Carl. And they left a good two hours ago, so they should be back soon. That way your dear old dad can go have a little nap in the back room."

Kevin yawned again, a bit more dramatically than the first time.

Lindsay looked horrified at the thought of standing guard over Carl, but Darcy knew her friend liked being helpful.

"Okay, sure," Lindsay said weakly. She took the syringe from Kevin and gave Darcy a look that clearly said, "Help me!"

Darcy glanced at her hot-pink watch. "I'd love to stay and help, Linds, but I have to get to rehearsal," she said apologetically. "But meet me afterward and we can go to Frannie Flynn's World of Fashion for fabric. Boy, that's a tongue twister!"

"Yeah, sure," Lindsay said distractedly as she took up her post next to Carl. She had her finger on the plunger of the syringe, and she was holding it just a few feet above Carl, ready to strike.

"Good luck!" Darcy called over her shoulder as she headed out the door.

Three hours later, Darcy was waiting outside the theater for Lindsay, furiously typing on her PDA.

❋ (DARCY'S DISH) ❋

Can things in Bailey get any weirder? you ask. Hello??? Of course they can! Take today, for instance. After lunch, Lindsay and I headed back to Creature Comforts to find Kevin babysitting a caiman! What's a caiman, you ask? Well, it's kind of like an alligator. They're still pretty huge. And this one was named Carl! Lucky for me, I had to get to rehearsal; otherwise, I might have had to help Lindsay and Kevin with the babysitting—um, I mean caiman-sitting.

Now rehearsal's over and I'm waiting for Lindsay so we can go fabric shopping. Here she comes now, and it looks like she made it through without a scratch. Gotta run! Later, gators!

❋   ❋   ❋   ❋   ❋   ❋

"There you are!" Darcy cried, happy to see Lindsay had survived her time with Carl completely unscathed.

"Ugh!" Lindsay exclaimed. "That was awful."

"Omigosh!" Darcy exclaimed. "Did Carl wake up? Did you have to inject him with the syringe?"

"No," Lindsay replied. "I'm just glad the whole thing is over. Carl was making me really nervous!"

"Well, if there's one thing that helps me calm my nerves, it's shopping!" Darcy joked. "So let's go!"

The girls headed to Frannie Flynn's World of Fashion, the only fabric store within a hundred-mile radius of Bailey. As they walked, Darcy told Lindsay that Ms. Harrington had been thrilled when Darcy had told her that Lindsay was volunteering to do the costumes for the play.

"She said she would be eternally grateful," Darcy said proudly. "Not a bad idea, if I do say so myself."

"Don't flatter yourself," Lindsay said wryly as she pushed open the door to Frannie's shop. The girls entered a tiny, cramped store that was filled with bolts of colorful fabrics stacked from the floor to the ceiling.

A tiny gray-haired woman peeked out from behind a pile of fabric that was at least twice her own height.

"Why, hello, dears," she crooned. "Let me know if you need any help."

"Thanks," Darcy replied. "We will."

Lindsay and Darcy squeezed their way down an aisle of fabrics.

"Ugh!" Darcy cried as a bolt of hideous faded metallic orange fabric slid off the shelf and landed in front of her. The other bolts of fabric surrounding the orange one weren't much better.

"I can't believe this place is called 'World of Fashion,'" Darcy whispered. "Has Frannie ever even left Bailey? Most of this stuff looks like it's been here since 1973!"

Lindsay pointed to a bolt of red-and-green plaid. "Well, that one isn't *too* bad," she said skeptically. "That might work for some of the men's shirts."

Darcy gasped. The plaid fabric was so ugly, it left her speechless.

"Lindsay, that fabric is so bad, I wouldn't even use it as a tablecloth!" Darcy finally said.

"It's just plaid!" Lindsay retorted. "What's wrong with plaid? It's a classic farm print. Farmers love plaid. Farm *animals* love plaid because they're used to seeing it so much."

"Lindsay," Darcy said, giving her friend a seriously severe look. "This is your chance to shine as a fashion designer! Don't limit yourself to plaids! Go with some-thing bold and different! The sky is the limit!" Darcy threw her arms up dramatically, looking upward at the towering shelves of fabric.

"Well, maybe not the sky, but definitely the top of that shelf!" Darcy added. "There's got to be some stuff in here that we can work with."

"But this play takes place on a *farm*, Darcy," Lindsay protested. "You can't just use whatever fabrics and patterns and designs you want—it has to be authentic!"

Darcy turned to face her friend.

"I think you're right," Darcy said.

"Really?" Lindsay asked skeptically. "You never give in that easily, especially when it comes to fashion."

"Well, I think you're somewhat correct," Darcy clarified. "I do think you have to be somewhat authentic, and the sketches you showed me earlier in the diner were totally farmlike. However, I don't see any reason why you can't take some creative license with the fabrics you choose in order to make those cute farm-style dresses and shirts."

"But Ms. Harrington—" Lindsay began to protest again, but Darcy cut her off.

"If Ms. Harrington can cast Oprah the llama as a lamb and Mini Me the ferret as a rat, then I think she's going to be okay with you taking a few liberties in your costume designs."

Lindsay thought it over for a minute. "You do make a good case," she told Darcy. Then a pretty floral print caught her eye. "And this print is a lot nicer than that plaid, even if it isn't one hundred percent authentic cowgirl."

"*Finally*, she sees it my way!" Darcy joked. "Now let's find some fabrics!"

By the time Darcy got home that night, she was exhausted. It had been a long day, from Carl to rehearsal to fabric shopping.

But even she had to admit that she wasn't as tired as her mother! Darcy entered the kitchen to find Victoria with her head down on the kitchen table—and she was snoring!

Every inch of counter or table space was covered in jars and jars of tomato sauce, pickles, and salsa. Each jar had a piece of masking tape on it that said "salsa" or "pickles" or "sauce." But Darcy noticed that a few of the jars were labeled with words like "picksa" and "saucles." Her mom must have been really tired!

Darcy leaned over and gently shook Victoria awake. "Mom," Darcy whispered. "Mom! You're snoring!"

"What?" Victoria asked as she bolted into an upright position. "I was snoring?"

Darcy nodded.

"Oh, dear," Victoria said. "Pickling and saucing is hard work! I'm exhausted."

"Mom, I think it's 'making sauce,'" Darcy said.

"Isn't that what I said?" Victoria asked dreamily.

"No, you said 'saucing,'" Darcy replied.

"Oh, a new word!" Victoria cried. "Lovely!"

At that moment, Jack burst into the kitchen, out of breath. "Hi, Victoria! Hi, Darcy," he said. His greeting was much more polite than usual, and Darcy was immediately suspicious.

"Oh, I'm so glad you're here, Jack," Victoria said. "All of the jars are sealed and ready to be stored in the basement."

"No problem!" Jack said eagerly. "I'm on it!"

With that, Jack scooped up an armload of jars and trooped off to the basement to deposit them.

"What's going on?" Darcy asked skeptically. "Jack Adams is helping you out?"

"Why, yes," Victoria explained. "He kindly offered to carry all of these jars downstairs to the cellar for me. Isn't that sweet?"

"Sweet?" Darcy asked skeptically. "I've never known

Jack to do anything sweet. You must be paying him a lot of money to do this, right, Mom?"

"Of course not, Darcy," Victoria said with another huge yawn. "Don't be silly. He volunteered. Now it's off to bed for me. See you in the morning, darling."

Victoria drifted out of the kitchen and upstairs, already half asleep.

Darcy sat down at the kitchen table and eyed the jars. She couldn't shake the feeling that Jack was up to something, but what could it be?

Darcy was sure it was only a matter of time before she figured it out.

Chapter 12

Wild Wisdom . . . *French poodles did not originate in France. Poodles were originally used as hunting dogs in Europe; their distinctive haircuts were to keep them from getting bogged down in water.*

It was opening night at the Bailey Playhouse, and the audience was packed. Strangely, everyone in the audience was wearing a funny hat. There were top hats and big wedges shaped like pieces of cheese. There were jester hats and baseball caps and ten-gallon cowboy hats. Darcy shook her head to be sure she was seeing correctly, but she was right—every member of the audience was wearing something strange on his or her head.

"Darcy!" Ms. Harrington yelled from backstage. "We can't find Petula's tutu!"

Darcy's stomach felt like there were a thousand butterflies flying around in it. *Oh, no!* Darcy thought. *How will Petula be able to tap-dance without her tutu?*

She ran around backstage looking in vain for the

123

The Play's the Thing

tutu while Petula tied on her tap shoes. Darcy was getting frantic. This was a disaster! How would Petula go on without her costume? The butterflies were moving up her stomach toward her throat. She couldn't breathe! Darcy felt like she was going to cry.

"Where's my tutu, Darcy?" Petula asked as she practiced a few shuffles and ball changes. "I want my tutu!"

That pig is talking to me, Darcy thought. *And I need to find that tutu!*

"Aaaaaahhhhhhhhhhhhh!" Darcy sat upright in her bed, screaming.

Victoria came running into Darcy's bedroom, a green clay mask caked on her face and tons of curlers in her hair.

"What is it, darling?" Victoria asked, alarmed. She perched herself on the foot of Darcy's bed.

Darcy took a few deep breaths. "Mom, you would not believe the dream I just had! Actually, forget about dream—it was a really crazy nightmare!"

"What on earth was it about?" Victoria asked. "Was it as bad as that dream you used to have when you were a little girl? You know, that one where your Rice Krispies would ask you math problems and geology questions, and then they would spit milk at you when you didn't know the answers?"

"Huh," Darcy said, suddenly reminiscing. "I haven't had that dream in a while, but I think this one was weirder! It was opening night at the play, and everyone in the audience was wearing a wacky hat. And then Petula was wearing tap shoes, and she was yelling at me because I couldn't find the tutu she was supposed to wear onstage. Ugh! It was just awful."

Victoria patted her daughter's hand. "There, there, darling," she soothed. "It was probably just an anxiety dream. You always used to have that Rice Krispie dream the night before a big test. And I'll bet you're just feeling nervous about the show because it opens next week. And this heat has been so terrible, I'm sure that's not helping."

The temperature in Bailey had been steadily rising over the previous week, and even with all of the windows open, the air in Darcy's room wasn't moving much. And it was so humid, she had given up trying to style her hair as the way she usually did. Instead, she had created an adorable updo that kept her hair off the back of her neck and was chic and stylish at the same time.

"Yeah, you're probably right." Darcy sighed. Then she suddenly became alarmed again. "The play starts next week? Omigosh! We'll never be ready in time. I have so much to—"

"Darcy!" Victoria snapped her fingers in front of her daughter's face. "Calm down. It's the middle of the night. The best thing for you to do right now is to get some rest. Believe me, I had many sleepless nights right before a big film shoot, and it certainly doesn't feel good the next morning. Just take a deep breath and go back to sleep. I'll bet you'll feel much better after a good night's rest."

"You're right," Darcy said sleepily as she leaned back into her pillows. "Thanks for the advice, Mom."

The next day at rehearsal, things weren't faring much better than they had in Darcy's nightmare. The air-conditioning in the theater was broken, and it was so hot, Darcy felt like she was at a sauna, not a play rehearsal! Ms. Harrington had set up a bunch of fans onstage to help keep the cast and crew cool, but the fans made it hard for her to hear everyone's lines.

"Jack, you need to speak UP!" Ms. Harrington shouted over the whirring of the fan.

"But I'm already shouting!" Jack yelled back.

"I KNOW!" Ms. Harrington replied. "But you're GOING to have to SHOUT LOUDER! Now begin again at the opening of scene four, please."

"Charlotte, do you really think Zuckerman will let me live and not kill me when the cold weather comes?" Jack said to Kathi. "Do you really think so?"

Kathi was white as a ghost, and she was wringing

126

her hands as she tried to squeak out her lines.

"O-o-of c-c-c-course," Kathi stuttered. "Y-y-you are a famous pig and you a-a-are a good pig."

Darcy and Lindsay were sitting in the wings taking a break and watching Kathi recite her lines.

"There's got to be something we can do to help!" Lindsay said desperately. "She looks petrified, and I know exactly how she feels. I'm having flashbacks to Carson City, Nevada!"

"I know," Darcy lamented. "She does look awfully nervous." Both girls hated to see their friend struggling so much.

At that moment, Ms. Harrington called for a water break. Kathi headed over to where Darcy and Lindsay were sitting.

"It's hopeless," Kathi cried as she plopped down next to her friends. "Apparently, the Charlotte in this production is destined to have a stutter."

"Oh! I have an idea!" Lindsay cried. "Isn't there an old trick where you're supposed to pretend that the audience is naked? I think it's supposed to take your mind off your stage fright and make it easier for you to say your lines."

"Yeah, I've heard that, too," Darcy agreed enthusias-tically. "My mom said she's used a similar trick on film shoots."

"Really?" Kathi asked, surprised. "Your mom? But she's a professional!"

"Well, yes, she is," Darcy agreed. "But even famous actors and actresses suffer from stage fright sometimes. My mom used to get really nervous when she was surrounded by a bunch of camerapeople and bright lights. She told me her secret was that she pretended all of the camerapeople were dressed up like apes. Worked like a charm!"

"Um, thanks, Darcy, but I think that just sounds like it would scare me," Kathi said hesitantly. "And I would try pretending the audience is naked, but I wouldn't even be able to see them from the sound booth where I'll be saying my lines."

"Hmm, good point, " Lindsay replied. "What if you tried picturing the cast and crew naked?"

"Yikes!" Kathi said, wrinkling up her nose. "The cast includes your little brother, in case you've forgotten! Plus, half of the cast is already naked—the animals don't have costumes anyway."

Suddenly, Darcy had the most brilliant plan.

"I know!" she exclaimed. "Lindsay, remember when you sketched that outfit for Petula as a joke? Well, that's what Kathi should do!"

"What? Take up drawing?" Lindsay asked, confused.

"I mean, it's a fun hobby, but I don't see how that will help with her stage fright."

"No, I mean she should imagine the animals wearing clothes instead of the other way around," Darcy instructed.

Kathi gave Darcy a withering look. "What am I supposed to imagine Petula is wearing?" she asked skeptically.

"I don't know," Darcy replied. "But you might want to start with a tutu and tap shoes."

The next morning, Darcy received an incredibly strange message from Lindsay on her cell phone. Kevin had ordered both of them to wear their swimsuits to work under their regular clothes. While Darcy thought it was a strange request, it had been so hot out lately that it sounded like a pretty cool idea—in more ways than one. So she put on her suit and headed to work.

She entered Creature Comforts to find the front of the clinic empty.

"Hello?" Darcy called out. "Anyone home? I'm dying to know why I'm dressed like a lifeguard even though I work at a veterinarian's office."

"We're outside in the back, Darcy!" Lindsay shouted.

Darcy poked her head out the back door of the clinic to find the entire Adams family—Lindsay, Kevin, and even Jack—wearing their bathing suits while they scrubbed down various animals.

"Well, this isn't exactly what I was expecting," Darcy said dryly. "I was sort of hoping there was going to be a surprise clinic trip to the water park or something!"

"Hi, Darcy," Kevin greeted her. "Got your swimsuit on?"

Darcy nodded.

"Well, then get to work!" Kevin said cheerily. "It's so hot, I figured everyone needed to cool off—humans *and* animals! And these two needed a bath, anyway."

Kevin tousled Jack's and Lindsay's hair as he spoke.

"Ha, ha, Dad," Lindsay said sarcastically. "You mean *these* two needed a bath."

She gestured toward the French poodle she was busy soaping up and the Labrador retriever that Jack was rinsing down with the hose.

Lindsay tossed Darcy a huge sponge and some rubber gloves.

"Why don't you start with Sammy here?" Lindsay suggested, pointing to the pit bull who was tied up next to the poodle.

He sure does look hot, Darcy thought as she looked

at the panting pooch. Once she splashed him with some water, he immediately looked happier.

"Hey, he really seems to like this!" Darcy exclaimed.

"Told you it was a good idea," Kevin said good-naturedly.

Darcy sighed. "If only it were this easy to cool everyone down at the play," she lamented. "Everyone's tempers have been flaring like crazy this week. I think it's a combination of the heat and the fact that opening night is just around the corner that's making everyone so irritable."

"Tell me about it!" Lindsay added. "I recruited a few members of your mom's Jaybird troop to help me sew the costumes while they earn their stitching badges, and they've been cranky all week. I know they're trying to help, but it feels like I've spent more time babysitting them than I have sewing! I'm so far behind."

"Well, girls, I'm sure everything will come together in the end," Kevin said reassuringly. "It has a way of doing that, if you haven't noticed. For instance, remember that night in third grade when you were panicking about finishing that Thanksgiving poem, Lindsay?"

"Wow, yeah," Lindsay recalled. "I remember that night. I was a wreck! I had writer's block, and I couldn't think of anything that rhymed with the word 'corn'! But you really calmed me down, Dad. You told me that I was doing a great job and that it was the best Thanksgiving poem you had ever read. Once I felt more confident in myself, I was able to finish it without a problem."

"Exactly!" Kevin exclaimed. "It's all about confidence. And I'm certain you girls both have what it takes to help make this play happen. I know it will all work out in the end."

"Thanks, Kevin," Darcy said. "It does help to hear someone else say that, especially after Oprah's performance at last night's rehearsal. She was spitting at everyone in sight! We couldn't even get through half a scene without one of the cast members running offstage to avoid being attacked."

"She must be feeling threatened, Darcy," Kevin said wisely. "You might want to try cutting down on the number of extra people that are around her while you're rehearsing those scenes. I'll bet if there are a lot of stagehands around in addition to the cast members in the scene, it's making her nervous."

"Good point," Darcy agreed. "I'll watch out for that tonight."

"Boy, you're full of wisdom today, Dad," Lindsay teased.

"Yeah, you sure are the smartest dad in the world," Jack piped up nonchalantly.

Kevin sighed wearily. "Yes, Jack?" he asked. "What is it that you'd like from me?"

"Whatdya mean?" Jack asked innocently. "I was just agreeing with my big sis about how you're the greatest."

Kevin gave Jack a look that said he knew Jack was trying to wheedle something out of him. There was no other reason for Jack to be buttering him up.

"Well, if you insist, I'd love to use the computer as soon as I'm done with this mutt," Jack hinted.

"Go ahead, Jack," Kevin conceded. "Now that Darcy is here, she and Lindsay can help me finish."

"Thanks, Dad!" Jack beamed. "You won't regret it. This new business venture of mine is going to make me—uh, I mean *us*—a fortune!"

And with that, Jack bounded into the clinic.

"What is this business venture Jack keeps hinting at?" Darcy asked suspiciously.

Kevin and Lindsay both shrugged.

"No idea, " Kevin said. "Whatever it is, though, he's been working on it for days now."

Darcy looked at Lindsay, eyebrows raised.

"I don't know, either," Lindsay scoffed. "He never shares his ideas with me because he's totally paranoid that I'm going to steal them. As if! None of his hare-brained schemes ever work out, so I have no idea why he thinks anyone—let alone a member of his actual family—would want to beat him to them!"

Darcy couldn't help but feel that Jack was up to something big. He'd been so suspiciously nice to everyone lately that he *had* to be up to something. But what was it?

Chapter 13

Wild Wisdom . . . *Ferrets, like skunks, release a scent into the air when startled or frightened. Luckily, a ferret's scent dissipates quickly and isn't as strong as a skunk's.*

It was the dress rehearsal of *Charlotte's Web*, two nights before the first curtain.

Darcy couldn't believe how quickly the show had arrived! Darcy arrived at the playhouse half an hour before the rehearsal was to begin to find Lindsay frantically rummaging through the costume bin backstage.

"Darcy!" Lindsay cried when she saw her friend. "Thank goodness you're here."

"Why?" Darcy asked. "What's wrong?"

"You won't believe this," Lindsay began. "I stayed up until three in the morning last night finishing Lizzy's dress for Fern so that she could wear it tonight for the dress rehearsal. Then the second she gets dressed, she decides she absolutely must have a box of fruit punch."

"Oh, no," Darcy moaned. "I think I know where this one's going."

"Exactly!" Lindsay cried. "There's fruit punch all over the front of the dress! I can wash it tonight after rehearsal, but the *Bailey Daily News* is planning to take photos for their theater review section during tonight's rehearsal. What am I going to do?"

"I'm sure we'll think of something," Darcy said as she rifled through the costume bin. She pulled out a short-sleeved white button-down shirt.

"What if Lizzy wears this white shirt over the dress, just for tonight? That way she'll still be wearing the bottom of the dress as a skirt, but this shirt will cover up the fruit punch stain on top."

"Brilliant!" Lindsay said as she hugged her friend. "Darcy, you are a fashion lifesaver."

"Why, thank you," Darcy said, bowing into a little curtsy. "Now, go! Save that costume!"

Darcy shooed Lindsay off and went outside to check on the animal trailer. First, she swung by Oprah's stall. The llama was relaxing, eye mask firmly in place. Darcy tiptoed over to the portable cassette player that was perched on a nearby shelf. She pressed "play," and a soothing nature sound track filled the stall. It consisted mainly of birds chirping and rushing mountain streams.

"There you go, Oprah," Darcy cooed. "Some meditation music to relax you before the big rehearsal."

Next, she checked on the goose, the gander, and the goslings. They were all chirping happily and munching on some grain that Darcy had scattered for them earlier that day. Their main role in the play was to just stand around in their pen, so Darcy really wasn't too worried about them.

After the geese, Darcy moved on to Petula. Darcy was pleasantly surprised when Petula came right up to her and nuzzled her leg.

"Awww," Darcy cooed. "Hey, Petula. Are you ready for the big night?"

Darcy waved a bright pink handkerchief in front of her, and Petula spun happily in a circle. Darcy thought Petula's curly little pink tail was wagging, but she knew that was ridiculous. But in any case, Petula did seem ready to perform.

Finally, Darcy checked on Mini Me. Layne had hung up photos of himself dressed as Dr. Evil all around Mini Me's pen to serve as inspiration for the little ferret.

"Ready to rock, Mini Me?" Darcy asked the ferret. "Do it for Dr. Evil, okay?"

Satisfied that the animals were all ready to perform, Darcy headed back into the main part of the theater.

"Hey, Darcy," she heard Eli's voice call out. She spun around, figuring he was behind her, but no one was there.

"Eli?" Darcy called back. "Where are you?"

"Up here!" Eli called from the rafters above her head. "I'm adjusting the lights, see?"

He held up a handful of colored gels that he had been busy placing over the lights.

"Be careful up there!" Darcy warned. The rafters looked awfully high, and the catwalk Eli was on was very narrow. "Are you wearing some sort of safety harness?"

"Yeah," Eli replied. "I'm totally fine. See?" He lifted up his arms to show that he was perfectly balanced, but then he began to wobble.

"Whoa!" he cried as he grabbed for the railing. "Guess I should hold on, huh?"

Darcy breathed a sigh of relief when Eli didn't come tumbling down on top of her.

"Yeah, that might be a good idea!" she agreed.

As Darcy was nervously watching Eli finish placing the light gels, Ms. Harrington arrived. Soon the rest of the cast and crew trickled in, and the rehearsal began. Darcy and Lindsay watched from backstage, where Darcy was in a prime position to coach the animals when necessary.

"I hope Kathi is able to get her lines out tonight without stuttering," Lindsay whispered to Darcy.

"I know what you mean," Darcy whispered back as she chewed her lip nervously. "I mean, tonight's the night! If she can do it now, she'll be fine during the play. I just hope some of our encouragement worked!"

Darcy and Lindsay watched as Kathi's first scene began. Petula was trotting around inside her pen as Jack belted out his lines as Wilbur the pig. Then Kathi began her lines.

"Do you want a friend, Wilbur?" Kathi said clearly. "I'll be a friend to you. I've watched you all day and I like you."

Kathi continued her lines, making it through the entire scene without a single stutter.

"Wow!" Darcy exclaimed when the scene was over. "That was incredible! Kathi was great."

"I know," Lindsay agreed with a nod. "Something must have really clicked for her."

Both girls couldn't wait to congratulate Kathi after rehearsal. When the play finally ended, Kathi raced out of the sound booth and bounded over to her friends.

"Did you guys hear me?" she shouted joyfully. "I didn't stutter at all! Not once! It was amazing. Thank you so much, guys. Your suggestions totally helped."

"Really?" Darcy asked, surprised. "Which one?"

Kathi started giggling. In fact, she started laughing so hard, she could hardly get the words out to explain.

"Darcy," Kathi gushed between giggles, "your trick really works. I'm not sure why you suggested I picture Petula in tap shoes and a tutu, but I tried it, and it was really funny. I was so busy trying not to laugh that I forgot to stutter! And then, during some scenes, it was fun to picture her in a tracksuit instead. And when Oprah came on, I imagined her in a tuxedo and top hat!"

Darcy and Lindsay joined in on Kathi's laughter.

"That is one of the silliest things I've ever heard," Lindsay admitted. "But I'm glad it worked! You were fantastic."

"Thanks!" Kathi said. "But thank *you*—both of you. I couldn't have done it without your encouragement."

"Well, why don't we head to the diner to celebrate?" Darcy asked. "I don't know about you guys, but I'm starving! I've been craving a veggie burger and fries all day."

"Mmm," Lindsay said. "I'm in. I could go for a chicken salad sandwich."

"Let's go!" Kathi chirped as she raced out the door.

Meanwhile, just outside the diner in the center of town, Jack was putting the finishing touches on his latest business venture, and Darcy was about to find out what he had been up to for the last few days.

When she, Lindsay, and Kathi emerged from the diner, they spotted Jack next to a folding table in the town square.

"Hey," Darcy said suspiciously. "What's Jack doing over there?"

Lindsay sighed. "I don't know, but I'm sure it's nothing good."

As the girls approached Jack, Darcy could make out pyramids of what looked like cans stacked on the table.

"Oh!" Kathi cried. "I know what he's up to. He must be collecting cans for the food drive. What a sweetie!"

"Sweet!?" Lindsay scoffed. "My brother is anything but sweet. And I'm fairly certain you'll see Petula sprout wings before my little bro helps out with a charity food drive!"

As Darcy approached the table, she saw that what she had thought were cans of food were actually jars—jars with her mom's picture all over them!

"Jack, what is going on here?" Darcy asked as she plucked a jar off the table. There was an enormous photo of Victoria Fields' head, and the jar read: "Victoria's Own Pickles."

Darcy glared at Jack. "You have got to be kidding me!" she exclaimed. "My mom made these pickles to enjoy throughout the long, cold winter, and you're selling them on the street?!"

"That's ridiculous," Jack scoffed. "The winters here in Bailey aren't *cold*."

"That's not the point, Jack!" Darcy cried, exasperated. "You can't make a profit by using my mom's image to sell the pickles and tomato sauce that *she* spent hours making!"

"Well, Newman did it, so I figured Victoria could, too!" Jack explained. "These things are going to sell like hotcakes! And anyway, your mom told me I could take as many jars as I wanted in exchange for helping her carry them all into her basement."

"Call me crazy, but I don't think she intended for you to take *all* of them and set up shop in the town square, Jack," Lindsay pointed out.

Jack sighed. "Does no one in this town have a sense of what it takes to be an *entrepreneur*?" he lamented.

"Oh, I do," a voice behind them said gravely.

"Uh-oh," Jack said, pulling nervously at his baseball cap. "Er . . . hi, Dad!"

Kevin strode over to the table and picked up a jar of tomato sauce.

"Hmm, original garlic tomato sauce," he read from the jar. "Sounds pretty good."

Jack thought he saw his escape window.

"Yeah, it is," he piped up. "And it's just $5.99 a jar, with ten percent of the proceeds going to support . . . uh, hungry kids in . . . Antarctica. Yeah, that's right. Antarctica! The winters there really are cold."

He glared at Darcy.

"Nice try, Jack," Darcy said.

Kevin put his hands on his hips, which Lindsay and Jack both recognized as his "I mean business" pose.

"Now, Jack," Kevin said, "why don't we head over to the Fields' house right now so you can tell Victoria how great sales are going."

"Uh, well, see . . ." Jack began as he nervously shifted from one foot to the other.

"She does *know* about this little capitalist venture of yours, correct?" Kevin asked severely.

"Well, she will now," Jack mumbled under his breath as he slunk off after Kevin.

"I knew it!" Darcy proclaimed once they had left. "I knew he was up to something. I just didn't realize it was something so . . . creative."

"That's my little brother," Lindsay said with a sigh. "Always coming up with a creative new way to scam someone—in this case, your mom!"

"Well, let's just hope my mom and your dad come up with a suitable way for Jack to repay her," Darcy replied.

"Oh, I'm sure they will," Lindsay said reassuringly.

Chapter 14

Wild Wisdom . . . *Ferrets are extremely social animals that frequently bond emotionally with other ferrets; in fact, bonded pairs are often observed to die just a few days apart from each other.*

When Darcy arrived at Creature Comforts the next day, she was in for a big surprise. Jack Adams was sitting morosely at a folding table in front of the clinic—the same folding table that had held jars of "Victoria's Own" tomato sauce and pickles the night before. Dangling from the front of the table was a handmade sign that read: "Help Feed the Children."

"Hi, Jack," Darcy said sweetly. "What's this? Another one of your get-rich-quick schemes?"

"Ha, ha, Darcy," Jack responded glumly. "This is my punishment. My dad said that since I was so interested in making money *and* in helping to feed needy children, I have to sit here every day for the rest of the summer until I'm able to raise five hundred dollars to donate to charity. Five hundred dollars! Do you know how long that's going to take? Forever!"

144

Jack hung his head dejectedly, and Darcy found herself actually feeling sorry for the kid. She dug around in her purse for some change, coming up with about $1.76, which she promptly dropped into Jack's bucket.

"Well, since it's for a good cause, I'm happy to contribute," she said cheerily. "And for the record, you might be more successful at getting people to donate if you didn't sit there looking like you're being tortured all day long. Come on, Jack, you're creative. Entertain people. That will make them much more willing to donate to such a great cause."

"Hey, you're right," Jack said, perking up a bit. "If only I had a clown costume. I could tell jokes for money! Or I could make balloon animals. Yeah! That's it. Thanks, Darcy!"

And with that, Jack rushed off to find himself some props.

Oh, no! Darcy thought. *What have I done? I can't believe I actually gave Jack another crazy idea!*

Darcy entered the clinic, ready to tell Lindsay all about how she'd actually helped Jack out with his punishment, but Lindsay was nowhere to be seen. Kevin was busy typing at the clinic computer.

"Good morning, Darcy," he greeted her.

"Hi, Kevin," Darcy replied. "Where's Lindsay?"

"Oh, she wasn't feeling well when she woke up this morning," he said. "She said something last night about chicken salad that made me think she may have a touch of food poisoning."

"Aha!" Darcy cried. "I knew that chicken salad looked fishy."

"Do you mean they gave her tuna fish instead?" Kevin asked, confused.

"No, I didn't mean fishy as in *fish*, but fishy as in suspicious and weird," Darcy replied.

"I see," Kevin answered. "Well, I'm sure she'll be feeling better soon. She didn't seem too ill."

"I just hope she's better by tomorrow night so she can be there for the opening of the play," Darcy lamented. "Her costumes look amazing, and it would be awful if she couldn't be there to see their stage debut!"

"Well, I'll certainly give her your best when I see her later," Kevin replied.

"Speaking of tomorrow night, would you mind if I leave a little early today so I can head over to the play-house to check on all of the animals?" Darcy asked. "I just want to make sure that Oprah has her meditation music on and that Petula has had her buttermilk bubble bath tonight!"

"Of course," Kevin replied. "You can take a break and head over there whenever you want."

"Thanks!" Darcy exclaimed. "I had a good feeling about asking you!"

"Oh, no!" Darcy cried. "I so do *not* have a good feeling about this!"

She was standing in the middle of the animals' trailer a few hours later, and something was terribly wrong. The Brennans had been inspecting the animals when Darcy arrived, and they had just announced that all of the animals seemed sick!

"I'm not sure what's wrong with them," Brandon said as he scratched his head. "They were fine this morning when I came by to bring Oprah this soothing, lavender-scented relaxation candle."

Darcy raised her eyebrows at Brandon. "Lavender-scented relaxation candle?"

"Well, you know she's a bit of a diva," Brandon said defensively. "I thought she might be nervous tonight."

Brett was inspecting Petula, who was lying listlessly on her side. Even Mini Me and the geese were unusually quiet.

Okay, don't panic, Darcy reminded herself. *The*

Brennans have a lot of experience with animals, and Kevin is still at Creature Comforts if I need him.

"Well, what do you guys think is wrong?" Darcy asked.

Brett looked completely befuddled. "Uh, heat exhaustion? It has been pretty hot outside these last few days."

"Yeah, but this trailer is air-conditioned," Darcy pointed out.

"Good point," Brett conceded. "That was my best guess. I really don't know what else would affect all of the animals at the same time like this."

Time to panic! Darcy thought. *Or at least time to get Kevin.*

"Okay, guys," Darcy announced. "You two stay here and make sure none of the animals get any worse. I'm going to get Kevin."

"Good plan, Darcy," Brandon agreed.

Darcy rushed back to Creature Comforts and practically dragged Kevin to the animal trailer, she was moving so quickly.

Once they arrived at the trailer, Kevin examined each of the animals. First, he studied Oprah and checked her heart rate and breathing. Then, he moved on to Petula. He felt her stomach and checked her eyes, ears, and nose. Finally, he inspected Mini Me and the geese.

While Kevin was checking the animals, Darcy was nervously pacing back and forth in the trailer, wondering what was going to happen. How had all of the animals managed to get sick at exactly the same time? She didn't think germs could have traveled from one animal to the next so quickly. Unless . . .

Suddenly, something caught Darcy's eye. She strode over to the corner of the trailer where the feed bags were stored. The sacks of grain and hay were sitting right underneath the air conditioner. Darcy leaned over to inspect the bags of feed, and she quickly noticed that the bags were wet. It looked like the air conditioner had been dripping on them.

"I'm afraid I have no idea what's wrong with all of the animals," Kevin announced as he put his stethoscope back in his bag.

"Um, Kevin," Darcy began, "you might want to take a look at this."

"What's that, Darcy?" Kevin asked. He strode across the trailer to the corner Darcy had been inspecting.

"Well, this feed is all wet," Darcy explained. "It looks like this air conditioner is leaking."

"That's a shame," Kevin said absentmindedly. "If it's wet and moldy, that whole bag of feed is ruined."

"That's too bad," Darcy agreed. Then suddenly she had another thought. "Oh my gosh! Kevin, I just thought of something. Can animals get food poisoning like humans?"

"Sure, they can," Kevin replied. "But what makes you think that's the problem?"

"You just said this feed was ruined because it's all wet, right?" Darcy asked.

"Well, yes," Kevin agreed, rubbing his chin with his hand. "I think I see what you're getting at, Darcy!"

Darcy lifted up the wet, moldy bag of grain. "Are you thinking that if the animals had eaten some of this grain, they might all have food poisoning, just like Lindsay?"

"Darcy, I think that's a very distinct possibility," Kevin commended her. "If that truly is the problem, the only think we can do is keep everyone hydrated and wait it out. There's no other cure for food poisoning."

"But what if they aren't all better by tomorrow night?" Darcy panicked. "What will we do?"

Kevin took a closer look at Petula and Oprah.

"They don't look too ill right now, so I have a feeling they'll all be fine by tomorrow morning," he reassured Darcy. "I'm sure they all just need some rest, like Lindsay. I checked up on her earlier, and she said after a nap this afternoon, she feels much better. I have a feeling it will be the same for your furry friends here."

"Whew!" Darcy exclaimed. "That was a close one!

That could have spelled disaster on opening night!"

"Really?" Brett asked jokingly. "I thought disaster was spelled 'd-i-s-a-s-t-e-r.'"

"Ha, ha," Darcy said wryly. "You know what I meant!"

Darcy leaned over to give Petula a good-night pat on the head. She really liked Petula, but there was no way this little piggy was getting a good-night kiss!

Then Darcy whispered some words of encouragement into Oprah's ear.

"Don't eat any more moldy grain, all right?" she told her. "And don't play your meditation music too loudly . . . the other animals have to get some sleep, too, you know."

"And so do you, Darcy," Kevin reminded her. "You've got a big day ahead of you tomorrow. Why don't I give you a ride home?"

"Sounds good to me," Darcy said with a big yawn. "I'm beat. Let's go!"

❋ ⟨ **DARCY'S DISH** ⟩ ❋

Ack! It's the night before *Charlotte's Web* opens, and you would not believe what happened. Lindsay and all of the animals got food poisoning from eating moldy grain. Well, Lindsay wasn't eating the grain . . . she had some bad chicken salad at Bailey's Hometown

Diner (the fries are still fantastic, though!). But the animals all ate the grain, and now they're all sick! Kevin seems to think all of the animals (and Lindsay) will be feeling better by tomorrow. Keep your fingers (and toes) crossed that he's right. If not, well, I'd rather not think about that!

Catch ya later!

Darcy shut her laptop and hopped into bed. She was exhausted from her long day, but somehow, she just couldn't fall asleep. As she tossed and turned, she tried her best to be optimistic. Still, she was really worried about the animals. What if they weren't feeling better in the morning? Without the show's stars, how would the show go on?

Chapter 15

Wild Wisdom . . . *The Patsy Award is given to an outstanding film or television animal trainer every year. "Patsy" is an acronym that stands for "Picture Animal Top Star of the Year."*

The next day, Darcy awoke to a beautiful, sunny day. She rushed downstairs, almost tripping over her pajama pants in the process.

"Good morning, sweetheart," Victoria greeted her. "Waffles or French toast? I'm cooking you an opening-day breakfast."

"Sorry, Mom," Darcy said apologetically as she slipped a pair of boots on over her pajama pants. "I've got to run down to the playhouse to check on the animals! If they're not okay, I don't know what we'll do!"

Darcy pulled on a sweatshirt as she rushed out the door.

"But Darcy," Victoria called after her, "you're still wearing your pajamas!"

"No time!" was Darcy's response as she sprinted down the driveway and hopped on her bicycle. As she pedaled down the driveway, she looked down at her pants.

"Eek!" she cried. "I'm wearing my pajamas!"

Victoria just shook her head as her daughter raced back into the house and back up the stairs.

In record time, Darcy was back on her bicycle, fully clothed. She pedaled furiously the entire ride to the playhouse. She had barely slept that previous night because she had been so worried about the animals. What if they were still sick? What if Petula couldn't go on? And what if Oprah was so listless, she couldn't make it out onto the stage?

She burst through the door to the animals' trailer and almost slammed right into Brett.

"Omigosh!" she cried. "Please tell me that every-thing is okay and everyone is feeling better!"

"Calm down, Darcy," Brandon told her. "Everything's fine. Everyone seems happy and healthy this morning. There's nothing to worry about."

Darcy slumped into the nearest chair with relief. Unfortunately, it was the chair that Brett had chosen as a resting place for a dish full of granola and yogurt.

"Ugh!" Darcy cried as she leapt back up. The back of her jeans was covered in yogurt and tiny bits of granola.

"Um, sorry Brett. I think I just sat in your breakfast. But thanks for letting me know that the animals are okay. That's a relief."

"No problem," Brett said. "I'm thinking I was done with that bowl of granola, anyway."

"Okay, good," Darcy replied. "I'd better head home to change now. Thanks, guys!"

A few hours later, Darcy's yogurt-covered pants were in the wash, and she arrived at the playhouse freshly scrubbed, wearing her favorite wrangling jeans, cowgirl boots, and pink cowgirl hat. She was even wearing a brown fringed suede vest to top the whole outfit off.

She headed backstage to find Lindsay frantically braiding Lizzy's hair. Luckily, all of the fruit punch had washed out of the floral-print dress she was wearing.

"Darcy!" Lindsay cried. "I need your help. Will you work on Lizzy's second braid while I finish this one?"

"You know, I *am* ten years old!" Lizzy cried indignantly. "I am perfectly capable of braiding my own hair."

"Of course you can," Darcy replied matter-of-factly. "But it's a well-known fact that braids always looks better when someone else does them for you."

"Darcy's right, Lizzy," Lindsay agreed. "I can braid

my hair, too, but whenever I want it braided for a special event, I ask Darcy or Kathi to help. They can see the back of my head a lot better than I can!"

"Okay, I guess," Lizzy mumbled. "That makes sense."

"Perfect!" Lindsay said as she tied a red bow at the bottom of Lizzy's braid. "You look great, Lizzy. Now, go break a leg!"

"What?!" Lizzy cried. "I don't want to break a leg! I broke my arm last year, and it really, really hurt."

Darcy stifled a giggle.

"That's just show business talk, Lizzy," she explained. "It's actually *bad* luck to tell an actress 'good luck' before she goes onstage. So instead, you're supposed to use the expression 'break a leg.'"

"Huh?" Lizzy asked, perplexed. "That makes, like, no sense!"

"Yeah, you're right," Lindsay conceded. "But that's what showbiz folks say when they want to wish someone luck before a big show. So, go out there and break a leg, but not literally."

"Gee, thanks," Lizzy said as she got into position for her first scene, still looking confused.

Meanwhile, the audience was beginning to arrive. Eli and Jack were busy handing out programs when Victoria and Kevin arrived.

"Good evening," Eli greeted them. "Can I show you to your seats?"

"Why, thank you, Eli," Victoria replied. "That would be absolutely lovely."

As Eli led Victoria to her seat, Jack sidled up next to her.

"Want to purchase a collector's edition program?" Jack asked slyly. "This one has all of the extras about the lives of each cast and crew member, as well as an exclusive interview with the show's director, and it's only five dollars!"

Jack tried to flash the program at Victoria while Kevin wasn't looking.

"Uh, thanks, Jack," Victoria replied, "but I think I'll pass."

She leaned closer to Jack so that only he could hear what she had to say next.

"And here's a word of advice for you," she whispered. "I wouldn't let your dad see you trying to sell those programs for profit when you're already in trouble for trying to sell off jars of my tomatoes and pickles!"

"Good point," Jack replied wisely, but it was too late.

"Ahem." Kevin cleared his throat loudly. "What exactly is going on over there?"

Kevin peered over his shoulder to spot Jack hastily stuffing the collector's edition programs into his back pocket while he continued to distribute the regular ones.

"Jack?" Kevin said. "What are you peddling?"

"They're just collector's edition programs for the show," Jack mumbled.

"And you're distributing them *for free*, correct?" Kevin asked.

"Uh, well, no," Jack said bravely. "When you go to baseball or basketball or football games, they make you pay for those programs, and they don't even have that much material in them."

Kevin glared at Jack, but Victoria just shrugged.

"Kevin, you have to admit that he has a point," Victoria pointed out.

"He may have a point, but he's still not selling those programs," Kevin said. He held out his hand to Jack. "Come on, hand them over."

"Aw, do I have to?" Jack begged.

Kevin raised his eyebrows. "The programs, please, Jack."

"All right." Jack sighed as he handed over the programs.

The lights began to dim as Kevin and Victoria settled into their seats.

"Oh, it's starting!" Victoria said.

Darcy peered out into the audience from backstage.

"Wow!" she whispered to Lindsay. "A lot of people are out there."

Lindsay peered out after her. "Yikes! A lot of people *are* here. I had no idea so many people lived in Bailey!"

"Actually, 1,678 people live here," Darcy told her friend. "And that's not including livestock."

"Wow," Lindsay said. "I'm impressed. Do you think all 1,678 people will come to see the play?"

"Anything's possible!" Darcy replied.

"That's for sure!" Lindsay agreed. "I never thought I'd get the chance to design and sew all of the costumes for this year's play."

"And *I* never thought I'd be a genuine animal wrangler!" Darcy exclaimed. "This has been one amazing experience. I'm surprised I had so much fun!"

"You know, Darcy, I'm really glad you helped get me involved with the play this year," Lindsay said shyly. "I would never have designed the costumes if you hadn't encouraged me."

"And I would never have known the animals had food poisoning if you hadn't eaten that chicken salad!" Darcy joked.

The two girls laughed.

"Well, I could have done without the food poisoning,

but this really has been one of the best summers ever," Lindsay said.

"Ditto for me!" Darcy agreed with a huge smile. "Now let's go on with the show!"

✳ (DARCY'S DISH) ✳

It's opening night! I know, I totally cannot believe it! Not only are the animals all okay, but the show is going really well. Actually, it's going so well that I'm reconsidering my future career as a Hollywood star. I mean, it's not like I wouldn't want to be a star, but this whole wrangling thing, well, it's not so bad (and I get to wear a cowgirl hat—how cool is that?). I guess what I'm saying is that I really like working with other people, but I think I'm starting to love working with animals. Turns out my first summer in Bailey has been one of the best summers ever!

✳   ✳   ✳   ✳   ✳   ✳